★

"How long was her body in the ocean?" I asked.

"Not long. There was dirt in her hair as if she'd been buried somewhere, then dug up."

"So she wasn't drowned? The reporting was vague." I knew why. Some details need to be kept from the public so that the killer might give himself away.

"There was no sea water in her lungs," Mac said. "The ME thinks she might have suffocated." Suddenly he asked, "You're not thinking of pursuing this, are you?"

I frowned. It wasn't good etiquette to get in the way of a police investigation. Still, it did seem as if our paths would cross. "It's so relevant to Edie Morrow's disappearance that I don't see how I can stay out of it."

★

"Complex enough to keep readers turning the pages... Who could ask for anything more?"
— *The Midwest Book Review*

Missing

Eden

WENDI LEE

WORLDWIDE.

TORONTO • NEW YORK • LONDON
AMSTERDAM • PARIS • SYDNEY • HAMBURG
STOCKHOLM • ATHENS • TOKYO • MILAN
MADRID • WARSAW • BUDAPEST • AUCKLAND

For Mari
This one's for you

MISSING EDEN

A Worldwide Mystery/February 1999

First published by St. Martin's Press, Incorporated.

ISBN 0-373-26301-5

Printed In U.S.A.

Acknowledgments

I would like to thank the following people for sharing their invaluable knowledge and support:

Barbara Puechner, Keith Kahla, Shawn Coyne and Dean Mudgett. Mari Famulari—I couldn't have gotten this book done without your knowledge of, and close proximity to, Boston, especially Eastie. Jack O'Malley, Boston private eye extraordinaire. Members of the Muscatine Aikikai: Dan Rohde, Brent Bowen, Josh Suderbruch, Randy McConnell, Bill Harris, John Ellis, Connie and Jake Young. Thanks for beating the information into me. My critique group: Mary Kay Lane, Dan Rohde, Rick Noel, Mary Campbell, John Deason—Matt Clemens and Judy Moresi. My friends who live too far away: Kim Fryer and Bob Wincott, Gaby Pauer, Deb Sorenson, Teresa Sisemore, Lea Farr and Mary Criquet, who keeps a T-shirt with a cover of *The Good Daughter* on display in her shop at the mall in San Mateo. My mentors, Max Allan Collins and Ed Gorman. My very patient husband, Terry Beatty. And a special thanks to a brilliant psychotherapist and good friend, R. Judith Vincent, M.A.C.P., and to Brent and Randy for their help with military facts.

ONE

I DON'T KNOW why the phone sounded different, more insistent, when I was outside my office, fumbling for my keys while balancing my coffee and croissant and a large package that I had found propped outside my office door. I'm sure the phone rang over ten times, but when I flung open the door, dropped my armload of stuff on the faded loveseat, and bodysurfed across the desk to pick up the receiver, all I got for my trouble was a dial tone. I cursed, mostly because my answering machine was on the blink again, and it meant calling Ma to find out if we have any shirttail relative who fixes this kind of stuff, or who might sell me an answering machine cheap. Not that I don't love Ma, but spending half an hour on the phone with her could drive even a therapist over the edge.

I looked wistfully at the phone, knowing I couldn't put it off much longer. I decided to spring for a new answering machine. My current answering machine only picked up messages when it felt like it.

My stomach growled, reminding me that I hadn't had breakfast yet. It was almost nine-thirty. I sometimes forget to eat during the day, especially if it's a day like today where I'll be doing some surveillance work for MassTix. Ticket scalping was on the rise at MassTix-related concerts. There had been so many complaints—and several pending lawsuits—that

MassTix management thought it was worth hiring me to find out which employee was buying up blocks of tickets and passing them on to scalpers.

I took a bite of my croissant—it was stale. As I was making a note to myself to bring along a sandwich, I also wrote a reminder that I had an aikido class tonight. I'm realistic about my work. There's usually not a lot of physical danger, but my first case was the stuff movies are made of—terrorists, the IRA, gunrunning, and bombs. Since then, it's been mostly car repos and insurance investigation claims. But during that first case, I was attacked, and although I was supposedly better equipped to defend myself than the average person, I ended up with a messed-up face. Still, the tenderest part was my bruised ego. So I looked into the martial arts, looking for a self-defense class that would teach me more than dropping to the ground and kicking my attacker in the knees and groin. I wanted to feel as if I was in control. Aikido seemed to fill that need.

I was staring at the large package I had picked up outside my door when the phone rang again.

"Hel-uh, Matelli Investigations," I answered smoothly. "How may I direct your call?"

A loud laugh assaulted my ear.

"Who is this?" I demanded in an indignant tone. I knew who it was—Sophia, my older sister—but I didn't want to give her the satisfaction of recognizing her voice.

"Ange, you got to work on that delivery."

"What do you want, Sophia?" I snarled.

"Well, aren't you in a good mood today. I just

called to ask if you wanted to have dinner at my place tonight.''

I stopped breathing. In our family, dinner usually meant dinner—unless you were invited by Sophia, whose idea of cooking meant taking the plastic film off the serving tray. This could only mean that she wanted something from me. When holding my breath didn't work, I closed my eyes and inhaled deeply.

''What do you want, Sophia?''

She sounded offended. ''What? I'm inviting you to dinner. Can you make it?''

I tried to come up with a reason to go to her place for dinner. I could see her kids—but I spent more time with them than Sophia did. I wouldn't have to cook for myself if I went to her place for dinner—but I had plenty of frozen dinners in my own freezer if I didn't feel like cooking for myself. I hedged. ''I don't know. I might have to work late. Why are you asking me?''

I could almost hear her shrug over the phone line. ''It's just a thank you, Ange.''

It was a thank you for introducing her to my friend Dave Whitney. Dave was my aikido instructor. My *married* aikido instructor. We don't have a lot in common, but we just hit it off. Sometimes those are the best friendships.

Dave has been going through a bad time in his marriage and he and his wife Pam are separated. He's a good-looking guy—tall and lean with a trim beard and warm brown eyes. I might have gone for him myself, but I don't do married men. Never have, never will. Not even if they're separated.

But Sophia and I are on opposite ends of the barometer on everything from politics to morals to lifestyles. When she was introduced to Dave at a party I threw a month ago, she latched on to him like a flea latches on to a dog. Not that Dave wasn't willing. Despite her hard life, Sophia is probably the best-looking of the Matelli sisters.

"By the way, Ma invited him to our family dinner next Sunday," Sophia burbled. "I'm a little nervous about it. So I'll see you tonight? I'm making my specialty."

"Yeah, I'll be there." Okay, so I was going to her place for dinner. It was just one floor down, and I guess I'm a little like an Italian-American Homer Simpson when it comes to food. There are certain things you should never tell me you'll do unless you're really going to do it, and one of those things is never, never tell me you're inviting me over for dinner and you're making your specialty—unless you mean it. Sophia's specialty, the only dish she made from scratch, was a northern-style lasagna. She added a nutmeg-flavored white sauce to die for. It was her saving grace.

Footsteps clumped up the hall, heading toward my office.

"Soph—" I was protesting as my office door was flung open and a worried Rosa came in. "I—I have to go. I'll see you tonight."

I hung up the phone and turned to my other sister. Sometimes I wondered if I should change the sign on the door to read Matelli Crisis Center and Hotline.

"Aren't you supposed to be in class, young lady?" I asked Rosa in a lighthearted way. She surprised me by bursting into tears. I got up and came around the desk to give her a hug. "Hey, I was kidding."

"I-I-kn-know," she snuffled. "But, oh, Sarge, I don't think I can go to school anymore."

I pulled my little sister to me and rubbed her back. My free hand reached out and found the box of Kleenex that I keep on my desk. "What's the matter? You want I should beat someone up for stealing your project or something?"

Rosa hiccupped, which turned into a laugh, and blew her nose. She sat up straight. "No, I mean it. I don't think I want to stay in school. I'm not sure what I want to do."

Well, it was true that Rosa had changed majors about as often as she had changed clothes in the past two years, but she was almost halfway through college, and she'd be the first one in our family to graduate. I was really rooting for her. In fact, I'd made sure that Rosa had a roof over her head and food on the table for the last year. When I'd bought a three-story walk-up that overlooked the East Boston harbor, I insisted that Rosa come live in one of the apartments as the "manager" so that I could justify her reduced rent.

My first instinct was to say, "Are you crazy?" Actually, it popped out before I could suppress it. Rosa looked up, tear-stained face, Bambi eyes. I hate it when she gives me those Bambi eyes.

"Don't start in on me, Sarge. Don't act like Ma."

I laughed. "Like Ma! Why, she'd be thrilled that you're leaving school. She'd fix you up with some nice Italian boy and be planning the church wedding right now. How many children do you expect to have? You might as well double it because Ma won't be happy till we're all married and popping out babies on a regular basis."

"Angie!" Rosa said sternly. She snuffled a little, and I handed her another Kleenex so she could blow her nose.

"What happened?" I said, sighing.

"N-nothing. I just, well, my adviser told me maybe I wasn't cut out to be an archaeologist."

"What the hell does he know?" I asked defensively.

Rosa glared at me. "Angie, he's the world's foremost authority on medical forensic anthropology. Why, he practically invented the subject." Having had a few years at the university, I knew that professors were their own best PR firm. Chances were that this professor had written a few articles on the subject when it was still an up-and-coming field, and it was to his benefit to proclaim to all who would listen that he had created medical forensic anthropology.

"Okay," I said slowly, "so what qualifies him as an expert on whether you should go into archaeology? Aren't anthropology and archaeology just kissing cousins?"

Rosa took a deep, shuddering breath. "I'd already been thinking that it might not be my field. But I guess hearing Dr. Winters say it made me feel...rejected."

I leaned back. Rosa had calmed down considerably. "But there are plenty of other things you can do, right? You have lots of credits. Why can't you just pick another major and switch?" I picked up the package and found my package cutter in the middle drawer of my desk.

She shook her head. "I can't do it that quickly. It takes time. I might spend another year or two at the U just taking classes for some other major that doesn't have similar requirements. I don't know what to do."

"Well, is there something you've had in mind, that you might be interested in?" I asked, feeling more like a job counselor than Rosa's big sister. "You could try something out for a little while to decide if it's what you want to do—you know, what's it called? Uh…" I made a clean cut across the taped opening of the package.

Rosa sniffled audibly. "An internship?" Her eyes were already brighter than they had been when she first came into my office. Maybe I wasn't so bad at this job counseling thing. I could do it on the side: Angela Matelli, Private Investigator, Therapist, and Job Counselor. Yeah.

"Yeah."

"Well, actually, there is something I've been kind of curious about," Rosa said in a soft voice—a soft voice that filled me with dread.

"What?" I asked in an equally soft voice. "What is it you're interested in?" I pulled the package open.

"Your job. I'd like to train with you as a private detective."

I had been about to pull out whatever was in the package, but her answer stopped me. I must have hesitated a fraction of a second too long. Rosa's shoulders slumped. "I knew you wouldn't want to have me work with you,'' she said in a miserable tone of voice.

"No, no," I replied a shade too quickly. "I think it's an…interesting idea. Ummm, let me think." I looked at my watch as a stalling technique. It wasn't that I objected to Rosa satisfying her curiosity, but I knew that if Ma caught wind of it, I'd be hung out to dry for "putting your little sister's life in danger." But maybe it would never come to that. I had the perfect case for Rosa to work on—so boring she'd be begging me to let her go back to school before the end of the day. And Ma'd be none the wiser.

TWO

THE MASSTIX OUTLET would open at eleven, and I had to be there at least an hour before that. "Tell you what," I heard myself say as I put the package to one side for the moment, "why don't you start today?"

She leaned forward, her eyes sparkling. "Oh, do you mean it, Sarge? I get to learn all about what you do?"

I forced a smile, feeling like a snake-oil salesman. "The truth is, this couldn't have come at a better time. I'm starting a stakeout in less than half an hour, and I didn't have anyone to share the duties with me."

The real truth of the matter was that Chuck Eddy, another PI who specialized in entrapping unfaithful spouses, would be dropping off his '73 Econovan at any moment, and I had been planning to ask him to drop by my surveillance spot in a few hours so I could take a lunch break. But the fewer favors I owed Eddy, the better. He and I had formed, at least on my part, an uneasy alliance. I wouldn't trust the man with the time. Eddy, on the other hand, was ever the optimist—always asking me out no matter how many times I'd broken his heart.

You know the saying, you can't judge a book by its cover? Well, in Eddy's case, the opposite was true. He looked like the sleaze that he was. He always had a scheme going. He had the hots for me, even though I'd made it clear that I wasn't interested. The words "Get your hand off my ass or I'll cut it off at the elbow, you sleazy asshole" would have felled a lesser man, but Eddy just thought I was playing hard to get. I didn't feel bad about using him whenever I needed something because I always made sure he knew he disgusted me. And he always managed to take it as a come-on. The man has a stainless-steel-plated ego.

I had just pulled the package back onto my desk when there was a breezy rapping on my pebbled glass door and, speak of the devil, Eddy walked into my office. Today, he wore an ensemble that would have given Mr. Blackwell nightmares: burnt-orange polyester pants and a black-and-white mock-houndstooth polyester jacket. The shirt, made of the stretchy, satiny polyester material so popular in the seventies, was a stained lime green. I blinked rapidly, hoping the psychedelic effect wouldn't leave spots dancing in front of my eyes for the next few weeks.

"Hey, babe," Eddy said, then chewed and snapped his gum. The smell of Juicy Fruit wafted past my nostrils. His sideburns were positively seventies, setting off his one continuous eyebrow. He held up a set of dangling car keys, which he tossed to me.

"Hey, yourself," I replied, nimbly catching the keys. "Wow, you're all dressed up. What's the occasion?" I had learned to keep a straight face around Eddy, but out of the corner of my eye, I could see Rosa was having a hard time keeping her thoughts to herself.

"I got a hot date."

"A hot date," I repeated like a mynah bird.

"Of course," Eddy said with a lascivious grin, "if *you* wanted to go out with me instead, I could call and cancel."

"Uh, no thanks, Chuck." What kind of girl wouldn't take it as an insult to be stood up? In Eddy's case, most of the female population.

He was already eyeing my sister. "Who's the chick?"

"My younger sister, Rosa. Rosa, this is Chuck Eddy, a fellow professional."

Rosa stood and shook hands solemnly. "Nice to meet you, Chuck."

Eddy looked her up and down, then glanced at me. I like to think that my warning glare was what kept him in line but, through no fault of my own, I had come to learn that Eddy likes his women a little more experienced. Fortunately, Rosa doesn't fit the bill. She's all wide eyes and innocence. "Nice to meet-cha, too, kid." He turned back to me. "I need the van back by the weekend."

"No problem," I replied. "If all goes well, you may get it back by tomorrow." I remembered the package in front of me and pulled out the contents, all wrapped in tissue paper.

"If you need the van to look official, I got a Department of Natural Resources sign in the back," Eddy said. "It's magnetic, so's all you gotta do is slap it on straight."

I didn't see how that would help me since rock concert tickets didn't fall under ecology, and I wasn't sure about the legalities of representing myself as a

government worker. But who was I to give Chuck
Eddy a lecture on ethics and the law when he was
lending me his Econovan?

The tissue paper ripped easily and, lo and behold,
a black lacy teddy festooned with little red ribbons
fell out. I gingerly picked up the lingerie by its straps
and held it aloft. Eddy gave a low whistle and raised
his eyebrow. "Nice stuff, Angie. You must have a
hot date tonight yourself."

I looked over at Rosa, who was suppressing a giggle. For the first time I looked at the address label
on the package. It was for the Romanian dentist
down the hall—who was a man. Hmmm. The possibilities were endless. Was it for his wife, his mistress, or was he a cross-dresser? In any case, I'd have
to retape it and put it outside his office door.

Before Eddy could get another word in, I thanked
him and, because he never knows when to leave,
ushered him out the door.

"Wow," Rosa said, "who was that throwback
from the seventies?"

"Chuck is an example of the fine quality of people
you will be dealing with if you decide to follow in
my footsteps." I grabbed my camera and my new
briefcase with the hidden video camera in it, and
made sure that both were loaded properly. I'd gotten
the briefcase at a discount through one of my numerous distant relatives who deals in mail-order spy
and technical equipment for people like James Bond
and me. My "uncle" had wanted to get rid of it
because this model had been discontinued.

I started to turn on my answering machine, then
remembered it was out of commission. I looked at

Rosa. "Say, my answering machine isn't working, and I really can't afford to miss any calls that might lead to other jobs. Maybe you could stay here to answer the phone while I stake out the MassTix box office."

Rosa groaned. "Oh, Sarge, that's so boring. I'd rather go on the stakeout with you. Can't you think of any other way?"

I glanced at my watch, realizing that I should be on my way there now. I didn't want to miss the employee who was the cause of MassTix's legal troubles because I was arguing with my sister over whether she should stay here or go with me. I decided to take a chance on the answering machine, and hit the "on" button. But I made a resolution to buy a new one before the start of business tomorrow.

We trundled down to the Econovan, which Eddy had thoughtfully double-parked and stuck an old parking ticket on the windshield, and took off for the MassTix office.

The MassTix outlet was located on Beacon Street just outside of Kenmore Square, on the way to one of Boston's tonier suburbs, Brookline. It was a slick storefront done in red, black, chrome, and glass, and the MassTix lettering was supposed to give the customer a feeling of fast service and reliability. There wasn't a parking space for blocks, so I drove the van down an alley opposite the ticket office and pulled as far over as was humanly possible.

MassTix's owner and CEO, Tom Caldwell, was also a concert promoter. When he had called me the other day for an appointment, I had wondered why he wanted to hire me. When I went in for the meeting, I was hoping for some glamorous job as body-guard to the Rolling Stones or something equally interesting, but instead I got the ticket scam.

"Ms. Matelli," Caldwell had started, being nothing if not politically correct, "for several years, I have been getting complaints from customers and potential customers who couldn't understand how they missed getting tickets to their favorite concerts. I always dismissed these letters as coming from people who didn't get to the box office quickly enough—until last week when I handled the upcoming Stones concert personally."

Caldwell knew that ticket scalping was a reality and was very, very wrong and had wanted to make sure the tickets got directly into the hands of fans. "But I was detained by other business and arrived an hour after the box office opened."

"Let me guess," I had said, "the tickets were already sold out."

Caldwell had gotten up and paced at this point. "Even accounting for sales over the phone in addition to the number of people lined up outside, waiting all night to get tickets, there was no way we could have sold out in an hour. We're talking about a concert at the Harbor Lights Festival." The Harbor Lights was a summer event, and the star attractions drew people from all over New England. Caldwell had narrowed his problem down to the Beacon Street outlet, but he didn't know which employee was dirty. I had easily checked their bank statements and also found out who recently bought a candy-apple red Miata. There were ten full-time employees handling the window sales at this outlet. At the moment,

MassTix was getting ready to put REM/Green Day tickets on sale.

I looked out at the MassTix storefront. The college crowd was already lined up, most of them dressed in plaid flannel shirts and baggy khakis.

"Is that what the up-and-coming college student wears these days?" I asked Rosa. I glanced at her thin cotton blouse and broomstick skirt.

She flipped her wavy brown hair back off her shoulders. Rosa had been growing it for the last several months and it looked good on her. "It's just one style, Sarge. We're not all alike, you know."

We talked about one thing and another, watching the students shuffle forward for an hour, paying for their tickets. Finally, an employee came out to get the attention of those who were still in line. I picked up my camera and got out of the van to get closer to the action.

The employee, a young man in his midtwenties, held up his arms. "People, I'm sorry to say that the REM/Green Day tickets sold out just five minutes ago." The crowd sent up a collective groan of disappointment and began to disperse, most heading toward the transit, or T stop across the street.

As a group of disheartened people walked by me, I heard one guy complain, "This is the third concert this summer that I haven't been able to get tickets to."

I pretended to be a tourist, taking pictures of the architecture, then slipping the camera down to street level once or twice to get photos of the employee who handled the crowd.

"Forty-five minutes? How could the tickets sell

out that fast?'' said one guy to his girl as they walked
by me.

"They're probably on-line now," said the girl. "If
you order by computer these days, concerts can be
sold out in a matter of minutes."

It was a nice theory, and at least the couple could
comfort themselves with that thought while they
missed the concert, but I happened to know that
Caldwell was only in the process of getting MassTix
on-line, and the system still had several bugs in it.

When I got back to the van, Rosa's arms were
crossed, she was slumped in the passenger seat.

"Bored already?"

"This is what you do all day? You just watch
people doing what they normally do and take pictures of it?"

"Well, sometimes," I allowed. "Other times, I re-
possess a car or investigate a health insurance
claim."

"What about that time you investigated that cop's
death? And you found out it was the daughter who
ultimately did him in?"

I smiled. "Cases like that don't come along all the
time."

She was prepared. Reaching back behind her seat,
Rosa pulled out a *Boston Globe*. She stabbed at a
small headline at the bottom of the second page with
her forefinger: 13-Year-Old Girl Found Dead in Revere.

"What about something like that? Why aren't you
investigating *her* death?"

I grabbed the newspaper and scanned the story. A
young girl's body had been discovered by two fish-

ermen early this morning on Revere Beach. I let out an exasperated breath. "Rosa, do I have to explain the fundamentals of private investigation to you? Someone has to hire me first, doofus. I wasn't hired to investigate that girl's death, tragic as it was. Besides, the police are undoubtedly working on it."

Rosa stayed silent for a while as I watched the front door. When I did the financial search yesterday afternoon, I had come up with the name of an employee—a Michael Elwar—who had amassed a considerable fortune in his bank account. I didn't know what he looked like, but I was willing to bet that the employee who came out of the door with something bulky like a briefcase or a backpack was Elwar. A few minutes before noon, four employees straggled out for lunch, most of them dressed casually and carrying backpacks or wearing bulky shoulder purses. But they all went across the street to a college-type deli. A few minutes later, a guy, tugging nervously at his tie, came out of MassTix with a backpack slung over his Arrow shirt. This was Michael Elwar. Bingo. I raised my camera.

"What are you doing?" Rosa asked, interrupting me.

I ignored her. My finger pressed the shutter several times. "Yeah. Come to mama," I muttered, lowering the camera and turning my attention to my pesky little sister. "What?"

She was staring at me. "You shot almost a whole roll of film on a guy who carries a backpack?"

I smiled sweetly. "Not just any backpack." Glancing at my quarry, I said, "Grab the briefcase. We're following him on foot."

The guy went two blocks, then entered a small Vietnamese restaurant. "This thing weighs a ton," Rosa grumbled as she followed me inside. "And I hate Vietnamese cuisine. They put lemongrass in everything."

"Pretend to like it," I said around the smile I had pasted on my face.

THREE

I ORDERED an appetizer plate of spareribs and some kind of lemongrass chicken and snow pea dish, and Rosa had some steamed pork dumplings.

Elwar sat alone at a table near us. Ten minutes passed before his contact joined him. The second guy was big—well over six feet, big hands, big feet, big face. Our guy had been fidgeting nervously over his tea, cradling his backpack as if it contained the secrets of existence as we know it. When the big guy approached, our guy, Elwar, frowned. He must have been cranky after his long wait. I tuned into their conversation as I sipped tea and nibbled a sparerib.

Rosa was spacing out, so I gave her a kick under the table. She jumped and glared at me. ''Pay attention,'' I muttered.

''Where've you been?'' Elwar asked.

''Sorry, Mike. I had a hard time catching the T from Arlington to Kenmore,'' the big guy explained. ''Then I had to hoof it from there. The cabs were all busy.''

Elwar let out an impatient sigh that came out like more of a petulant snort. ''I don't like to be kept waiting.''

''Too fuckin' bad,'' the big guy said in a placid tone. ''You got the goods?''

Elwar leaned over and said in what he thought was

a low and dangerous tone, "Don't use that term. We agreed to keep this exchange as—"

The waiter interrupted to take their order, and Elwar switched back into a normal tone as if he had this kind of rendezvous all the time. When the waiter was gone, he leaned back toward the big guy and continued in a low voice as if nothing had happened.

I didn't get a chance to do much more than finish my sparerib before they got up from the table, throwing money down for the waiter's trouble. I hoped that the video in the briefcase was recording the meeting clearly. I was pretty sure my word would be good enough, especially with a second witness, Rosa, to call on, but it didn't hurt to have a witness as impartial as videotape.

The big guy took the briefcase from the soon-to-be ex-MassTix employee, and I decided we should lose Elwar and tail him. I paid the bill quickly, not waiting for my change, and Rosa and I followed the big guy, whose name we learned when he entered a brownstone off Arlington Street.

"Richard Tallman," Rosa read out loud. "That can't be his real name, can it?"

"Very Dickensian," I murmured. My sister looked at me, wide-eyed. I smiled at her. "Don't look so surprised. I may be ex-military, but I'm not some grunt who never read a book. As you may have noticed, I'm not dating much these days."

"I thought it was awfully quiet up there," Rosa replied with a grin.

I shrugged. "Yeah, well, we better finish this job. I think we've gathered enough evidence for our client to fire this guy and keep him out of the concert business for years. Let's get back to the office.''

The answering machine was blinking, which meant it had either picked up the message in its entirety or that it was teasing me with half a message. Over the past week, I can't count the number of times I ran through message after message that ended with "Call me at—BEEEP.''

I held my breath and punched the playback button. The machine whirred, and a male voice began to talk. "Angie, this is Everett Morrow. Do you remember me? I want to hire you. Meet me at two o'clock at the Bell—BEEEP.'' Oh, great. There's a job down the toilet.

Rosa snickered behind me. I sighed deeply and slumped into my chair. "Damn, Ev and I used to work together. Bell what? Bell Tower? Beltronics? I wish I'd bought that new answering machine this morning.''

Without saying a word, Rosa reached for the phone book that I kept on the corner of my desk and started paging through it.

"Ball One,'' Rosa flipped a couple of pages and ran her finger down another page. "Belknap, Bella... here,'' she stabbed the open yellow pages with her finger and shoved it at me. "The Bella Restaurant at two.''

"Hmmm, maybe you *should* be a private eye,'' I said as I checked my watch, noting that I had twenty minutes to meet Morrow. "Now for your first solo assignment''—Rosa leaned forward eagerly—"you can write up a report of our surveillance today.'' As I stood up, Rosa groaned.

"Can't it wait?" she pleaded. "I'd like to go with you to meet this guy. I might miss something."

I grimaced. "It's probably nothing more than a peeper case."

"A peeper case?"

"Where the client wants the spouse followed to see if he or she is having an affair," I explained. "Along with insurance claims and repos, it's my bread-and-butter."

"Well, if I had my own detective agency, I don't think I'd do that sort of work," Rosa said with the truly naive spirit I'd had a year ago—that is, until I found myself playing poker with imaginary friends during those long stretches when insurance and repo agencies didn't have the extra work to farm out to freelancers like me. I got really good at poker, but it didn't bring in the mortgage, so I stopped turning away peeper cases.

"Besides," I said as I headed for the door, "it's better to get the report down on paper while it's fresh in your mind. And please take messages while I'm out. I'll return calls from potential clients."

Before she could protest again, I slipped out and headed down the hallway for the elevator.

I WAS ONLY five minutes late for the meeting, so I took a moment outside the Bella Restaurant to catch my breath. I'd jogged all the way there. The Bella Restaurant is located on the edge of the North End near Haymarket. It's a popular place with tourists and my guess was some out-of-towner who had been there while on vacation had recommended it to Ev Morrow, who is not a native Bostonian. Frankly, out of all the people I'd known in the marines, I was most surprised that Ev, my superior for my first years in the corps, was the first one to call me.

Not that I wasn't happy to hear from him. I had been his driver, and Ev had been the one who had gotten me transferred to the Special Investigations Division of the MPs. In essence, Ev Morrow was responsible for my career, if you could call being a PI a career. Ma might not be so happy to meet Ev, but I have to say I'm still grateful. Of course, the reason he got me a transfer had nothing to do with my driving record—it had more to do with the fact that we were attracted to each other as more than friends and that he was married.

The few times Ev brought me home to his family, I had tried to get along with his wife, Earlene, but she made it difficult for anyone to like her. Earlene was a lush who started her day out with a Bloody Mary, and she was paranoid about losing Ev. I think the final straw was when she accused me of having designs on her husband. While Ev was an attractive man, and one I wouldn't have thought twice about going out with if we weren't working closely together, I've always had an aversion to dating married men, especially when they're my superiors.

Ev had been embarrassed both for me and for him and tried to joke about it the next day, but it'd been clear that the only recourse we had—considering that Earlene had hit uncomfortably close to home—was for him to request a transfer for me. That had happened seven years ago.

I took a deep breath, hoping that Earlene wouldn't be there to make the meeting uncomfortable, and

walked in the door. Even though seven years had
passed, Ev was still easy to spot: over six feet tall
with a great build and a jawline you could cut a
diamond on. His sandy hair was a slightly longer
version of the haircut worn by the marines. He'd
been a good-looking man when I knew him back
then, and seven more years of experience had only
made him more attractive.

I was surprised by the way he was dressed—dark
blue suit, pale-gray shirt, and a narrow, red-patterned
dark-gray tie. The last time I'd seen Ev, who was
then a major, he'd been dressed in his B uniform,
the step down from our dress blues. I wondered if
he'd been promoted. As he looked now, he could
almost pass for a civilian, except with those of us
who were trained to recognize a fellow marine.

He was seated at a table, nursing a cup of coffee.
When I caught his eye, he stood up and smiled. As
I got closer, I noticed that although Ev seemed happy
to see me, there was a reserved air about him—this
from a man who had once shared dirty jokes with
me. But it had been a long time, time enough to make
a good friend a good acquaintance.

I extended my hand, and he clasped it firmly in
both of his, pumping my arm up and down as if he
were expecting me to spout water at any moment. A
whiff of Ev's woodsy cologne drifted past my nose
and I inhaled deeply. The scent reminded me of pine
forests and clean mountain air.

"Angie, good to see you."

I felt my lips part and spread over my teeth in
something resembling a smile. "Good to see you,
too, Ev. It's been, what, seven years?"

"Five. I think the last time I saw you was at that Christmas party over at the Yuma PX." I remembered. Earlene had been there, drinking too much and making an ass of herself. She'd made it clear she thought I had orchestrated this chance meeting with Ev. The fact was that I was surprised to see him there. We had both been reassigned to other military installations.

I glanced at the table, noting there were only two place settings, two glasses of water with thin, round slices of lemon floating among chunks of ice. "Sit down. Order something, if you're hungry."

I realized that I hadn't eaten much today. No breakfast—my croissant was still sitting on my desk uneaten—and my working lunch had been interrupted by the two jokers I'd had under surveillance. So when the waiter came to take our order, I ordered the veal scallopine and a glass of Napa Valley zinfandel. Ev had another cup of coffee.

"What've you been doing with yourself?" I asked.

He shrugged. "I was promoted to lieutenant colonel since we last saw each other."

"Congratulations. Where are you stationed now?"

He shook his head. "California."

"Twenty-nine Palms?" Twenty-nine Palms was a desert-based training ground for the corps.

"No. I'm working on a project that I can't talk about."

Hmmm. I knew enough not to ask, but I could read between the lines. He was probably working for the Department of Defense.

I changed the subject. "From the message, I take it this is not a social call."

He smiled again, but I still got the feeling that there wasn't much enthusiasm behind the smile. "You're right. I suppose we'd better get down to why I called you. I want to hire you to find my daughter, Edie. She's been missing almost three months."

FOUR

I HAD TO LET that sink in. When I'd known Ev and his family, Edie'd been about seven years old. I had liked her—she had been a quiet, almost adultlike child. Most military brats tended to be either very quiet and studious or they rebelled. It wasn't uncommon for a quiet child to rebel years later. Today she'd be about fourteen, which was a difficult age. I wondered if she had run away.

Before I could speculate any further, Ev began to talk. "I got rid of Earlene, Angie. Divorced her, I mean—although killing her would have been too good." He took out a photo from his wallet and handed it to me. "This is the most recent picture of Edie."

I remembered Eden Morrow as a bright, imaginative seven-year-old girl, the light that shone in her daddy's eye. I remembered spindly arms and legs, knobby elbows and knees, inquisitive brown eyes, and fair hair like her dad's. Edie, a nickname for Eden, hadn't carried a Barbie doll like other girls her age—instead, she had a blond G.I. Joe. Whenever someone would ask her his name, she'd reply, "Phil Inn." Ev had given it to her one day when he had to go away for four weeks.

The photo had creases and soft edges as if Ev had taken it out again and again to stare at it, to memorize the lines of the face so he wouldn't forget. It showed an older version of the Edie I'd known. I could see some of Ev's features in his daughter—the same strong chin and high cheekbones. But the brown eyes and the generous mouth were her mother's. The long, blunt-cut hair was a light gold, the color of newly sprouted wheat.

Edie wore a blue-and-red plaid jumper over a high-necked white blouse with ruffled collar and cuffs. Her hair was neatly combed and tucked behind the ear that faced the camera. She wore two pierced earrings—a small gold hoop and a diamond stud. I guess it was a modest rebellion against convention. Of course, I had three piercings in one ear, so I shouldn't have been too surprised.

I studied the photo, hoping it would give up some secrets. Edie stared back at me, her smile a bit sad, her eyes serious. She was going to be a beautiful young woman.

"You've done well, Ev," I said when I looked up from the photo. "She looks like she's turning out fine."

Ev allowed himself a small, proud smile. "She's bright, too. Not straight A's, but a three-point-five average. The only class she struggles with is history. She just gets bored."

"Mine was geometry," I admitted. "No problem with calc or algebra, just all those lines and stuff." I took a sip of coffee. "Tell me about the divorce."

"The judge granted custody to me and limited visitation rights to Earlene because of her past history with the bottle."

"As I recall," I said, "Earlene was never much of a mother."

Ev looked down at the tablecloth and shook his head. "She never wanted Edie. She went for custody because she wanted to get back at me, not because of any maternal instinct."

While these could be the words of a bitter divorced man, I knew differently. I knew Earlene—not well, but well enough to know that he was speaking the truth.

It wasn't that Earlene was a bad person, she had just always been immature and scared. Ev had once told me about Earlene's background: She had never known her father, and when she was ten, her mother had abandoned her and three younger siblings. Earlene had taken care of her brothers and sister for almost a week before a neighbor noticed that an adult hadn't been around the house for a while. Then the social workers descended, separating the children and sending them to different foster homes, never to see each other again.

It was a sad story, one that made me understand Earlene's insecurities, but I had known people with far worse backgrounds who were now successful and well-adjusted. I guess I just get impatient when I see someone wallowing in a tragic past, not being able to get on with their life. I think it's a waste.

"Three months is a long time, Ev. I assume that you think she's with Earlene."

He nodded. His hands were wrapped tightly around the cup of coffee, and before he could continue, my meal was placed in front of me. I suddenly felt as if I'd committed a faux pas by ordering a late lunch while this man told me about his missing daughter. I started to apologize, but he waved it away. "I'd like to tell you the story; then you can decide whether you can do anything for me."

While I whittled away at my rubbery scallopini, Ev told me about the painful custody battle, about the things Earlene did and said to try to poison Edie against him.

"The divorce went through about two years ago. It wasn't hard to prove that she was unfit, what with her drinking and those public demonstrations of affection to strangers. There were people only too happy to testify on my behalf. Outside the court, as I was taking Edie to the car, Earlene came up to me and told me in a low voice that she would get me back."

Ev was then transferred to Guam and stayed there for a year and a half. "It wasn't hard to keep an eye on Earlene when she came to visit. She was flown in by military planes and flown out again. Edie was really happy there, and I thought we might be in for a long stay."

But eight months ago, Ev had been transferred to California. "Edie began attending a public school. She had a hard time fitting in, as any child would have who hadn't grown up with all those kids, but she seemed to be doing all right. Then Earlene went back to court and got a judge to grant her unsupervised visitation rights. Right after that, she came by one day unexpectedly. Said she was visiting nearby friends, thinking about settling in the area and getting a job so she could be near Edie." Ev paused and sighed, running his hand over the back of his head as if he could wipe away all the bad memories. "She was so civil, so friendly that I thought maybe she'd changed. Maybe she'd stopped drinking, even. I was happy for her."

"So against your better judgment," I interjected, "you let her take Edie on a trip to Disneyland or someplace like that."

Ev's smile was bitter. "Actually it was Magic Mountain, a favorite of Edie's."

"They never came back?" I asked.

"I asked around at Magic Mountain, talked to the employees who worked on the day Earlene was supposed to take Edie. No one remembers them."

"And for the last three months, you've heard nothing, found no one who might lead you to them?"

Ev stared at his empty cup as if willing coffee to magically appear. The waiter must have had a sixth sense because he seemed to come out of nowhere to give Ev a refill. I glanced at my half-eaten meal before pushing my plate aside. Suddenly, I wasn't hungry anymore.

I was starting to wonder where this was leading. What was my role? Was I supposed to pick up the gauntlet for Ev and criss-cross the country in search of his missing daughter and ex-wife?

"Angie, I'm worried sick. I haven't slept well since she disappeared." Ev raised his eyes to meet mine. "I've spent every free moment I've had working on finding them. I hired private investigators on the West Coast, and I worked on sending out fliers to every possible lead out there. It was as if Earlene and Edie vanished into thin air."

I kept my thoughts to myself. The investigators he'd hired couldn't have been very good. Although it was possible to disappear without a trace, you had

to cover your tracks for months before, and you had
to be smart. Earlene didn't have the patience to plan
something like this, and she wasn't smart enough to
pull it off. Not unless someone was helping her.

Ev looked down at his hands. "Last week, I got a
phone call from Edie, a collect call."

"Did she tell you where she was?"

"We didn't have a chance to talk—Earlene must
have caught her and we were disconnected." Ev
shifted in his seat. "I didn't want to wait for my
phone bill to show up to find the number, and I have
a few friends with connections at the phone company. So I was able to find out where the call had
come from. It was a phone booth near someplace
called Lechmere."

Lechmere was a T stop in Somerville. The area
around the T stop had housed small businesses, abandoned and condemned buildings, and a large, Kmart-
like store for which the stop had been named.

Urban renewal was slowly creeping over the entire
area. There was now a nice mall called the Cambridge Galleria, which had interesting little stores and
eateries.

I focused on Ev again. "But that's all you came
up with."

He leaned forward and clasped his hands together.
"I know they're in this area now, and I want to hire
you to find them. I want my daughter back. Angie,
you'd think that I would have felt some relief that I
heard from her and that I know now that she's with
Earlene. But I can't help feeling that something terrible has happened to her, and it's driving me crazy."

I was silent for a minute, turning it over in my

mind. This would be a difficult case with all the time that had gone by. On the other hand, Edie was still alive, unlike the girl whose body had been found on Revere Beach.

"I can't accept your money," I said.

Ev leaned forward, looking into my eyes. "You know I've never asked you for a favor." He added in a low tone, "And under normal circumstances, I would never put pressure on you by reminding you that you wouldn't be a PI if I hadn't gotten you that transfer to the Special Investigations Division—"

"Please, Ev, you don't have to—"

He went on as if I hadn't spoken. "—but I'm desperate—"

"Ev, I didn't say I wouldn't take the case."

He blinked. "You didn't?"

"No, I said I wouldn't accept money. I'll work for you, but as a friend."

He lowered his eyes, looking at his hands again. "I can't let you do that."

"Then give me a dollar and we'll make it official. And you'll pay for business expenses."

He seemed to be thinking this over for a moment, then nodded curtly and decisively. We shook hands, he paid the bill for the meal I almost ate, and we left the restaurant.

Ev and I parted, but not before he promised to drop off the information he'd gathered from his own investigation and the reports from the California private investigators who had worked on the case. "I probably won't be able to get the information to you before tomorrow morning," he warned me.

"That's okay," I replied. "I won't start on the case until I've gone over the files."

When I got back to my office, Rosa was gone, a neatly typed report on my desk of this morning's activities along with a note telling me that Sophia had called, desperate for a babysitter so she could work an early shift. I knew that Rosa must be getting disillusioned with PI work already if she left my office to rescue our narcissistic sister. I would have to have a talk with Rosa.

FIVE

WHEN I GOT TO THE DOJO, I changed into my *gi* and *hakama,* took off my shoes, bowed onto the mat and sat *seza*—legs tucked under in a position that, in the course of five consecutive minutes, would have my calves and feet totally numb. Milt Koenigsaecker sat next to me. "Missed you the other night," he muttered just before our *sensei,* Dave Whitney, bowed onto the mat and sat *seza* front and center.

"I worked late," I muttered back. Then we bowed toward the image of O'Sensei, decorated with silk flowers on either side. A rack of *bokken*—wooden swords—and *jos*—straight sticks about three feet long—flanked the shrine.

Yeah, I know it sounds like a bad scene from a Chuck Norris movie, but I'd started taking aikido a few months ago and was just discovering how totally incompetent I am at self-defense. Sensei turned, and we bowed to each other; then we began stretches and warm-ups.

The problem with most martial arts, in my opinion, is that they are usually a good place to meet psychotics and sociopaths. Not that all practicing martial arts students are sociopathic, but if you were looking to meet a sociopath, a martial arts class is a good breeding ground. Aikido is only a little over fifty years old. When I was looking into the martial arts, I was impressed by the fact that the founder of aikido was practicing right up into his eighties, about a year before his death, and he hadn't even begun to create aikido until he was well into his forties.

Aikido uses sword techniques, throws and pins, relying on the momentum of the attacker. It takes longer to learn than a one-day women's self-defense workshop, but I think it has a more lasting effect.

Toward the end of class, when the sweat was running cold down the back of my neck and I was breathless from the workout, Sensei partnered up with me. "How you doin', Angie? Didn't see you at class last Thursday night."

"Had to work," I explained as I executed a *ko-dagaeshi,* one of my best techniques, if I do say so myself. Sensei did a break fall, slamming into the mat with the full force of his body. I flipped him over and pinned him, *nikkyo*-style, with a knee on either side of his shoulders and his arm lifted up and pinned at the elbow and the wrist.

He slapped the mat to indicate it was a good pin, and I let him up. I held up my hand and began to adjust my *hakama,* the black split skirt worn by men of black-belt rank and all women. I had never learned to tie it right.

As I tightened the sash, I grinned and said, "I'm having a bad *hakama* day." Sensei groaned.

After class, Sensei—Dave, now that class was over—caught up to me as I headed out of the building. When he wasn't teaching aikido, he was a child psychologist.

"You drive here?" he asked.

I shook my head. "I took the blue line to the orange line."

"I'll drive you home, then." I must have given him a strange look. After all, he lived in Dorchester. He shrugged. "I'm not in a hurry to get home," was all he said. I understood. If you were used to coming home to somebody, it would be hard to get used to being alone.

Dave saw the lights on in Sophia's place. "I see she's home." His eyes were bright, a smile on his face. I might have thought it was kind of sweet if this wasn't the night Sophia was making her lasagna for me. I didn't feel like sharing.

"Uh, yeah." I shifted uncomfortably in the passenger seat. "You're welcome to come in, Dave. But I have to warn you, I think Sophia wants to talk to me alone tonight. It may have something to do with family." It usually does.

"Oh, I understand," he said too quickly, his expression reminding me of a lost puppy dog. I hate that expression. I always want to slap the person silly and tell them to snap out of it. "I'm seeing her tomorrow, anyway." He bid me good night and drove off toward the East Boston Expressway.

The smell of oregano, basil, and tomato sauce had drifted into the hallway outside of Sophia's apartment, reminding me that I was starving. Sophia opened the door. "The kids are up in Rosa's place already. Come on in. I saved some for you."

It figured. She hadn't waited to eat with me, which meant she was going to ask me for a favor. I had already rented this ground-floor apartment—the smallest of the three—to Sophia dirt cheap, with the understanding that she continue to look for a more suitable place to live since the ground-floor apartment had only one bedroom.

When Sophia and her brood had moved in, we converted a large walk-in closet to accommodate Michael, but Stephanie had to sleep with her mother, or on the fold-out couch if her mother had company. Neither situation thrilled me—I didn't think it was healthy for either kid.

It wasn't that I didn't love Sophia, but we hadn't been able to live under the same roof when we were growing up, and I had worried about her being here. But it had actually worked out for the best. Sophia considered all of our apartments to be extensions of hers. She worked nights at a bar and left her kids with Rosa and me. Our spare bedrooms were second homes to Stephanie and Michael.

Sophia set down a steaming platter of northern-style lasagna, fresh steamed broccoli with garlic, and bread dripping with garlic butter in front of me. As I attacked it, she sat down opposite me with two glasses of red wine.

"You must be hungry," she said tentatively.

"Mmmm," was all I could say around a mouthful of garlic bread. She smiled. I noticed that her skin was dewy, almost glowing. I stopped chewing and managed to say, "You're not pregnant again, are you?"

Her eyes narrowed. "What the hell made you ask a thing like that?" She took a big swallow of wine, downing almost half the glass. A moment later, her expression cleared and she shook her head. "You don't have to worry about that, Ange. I know I'm not considered the responsible one around here, but I'm not that stupid.''

I ducked my head, almost feeling sheepish about having asked her. Then I took a bite of her lasagna. "God, this is good, Soph. You should really consider opening a fast-food lasagna place. The only item on the menu would be this lasagna with all the trimmings. It's heaven.''

Sophia beamed. It was the one thing she was proud of, with the exception of Stephanie and Michael.

Then she sobered a bit and got to the point. "Ma's invited my new boyfriend to dinner this Sunday.''

"I know that," I replied, catching the last drop of red wine in my glass. Sophia was there to fill up my glass so fast, I knew something was wrong. "I also know he's still married and a good friend of mine. So what's the problem?''

Sophia refilled her glass as well. "I haven't told Ma about his marital status yet.''

"Well, duh," I said, wiping up the last of the cheese and sauce from my plate with a hunk of garlic bread. "When are you going to tell her?" I took a large swallow of red wine.

She sighed and starting toying with her wine glass. "I thought you might do that. Dave is your friend, after all.''

I almost did a spit take, then thought better of it and tried to swallow. But it went down the wrong way and I started to cough, pounding my chest while Sophia got me a glass of tap water. I drank the tepid stuff and took a few deep breaths.

She sat near me, oblivious to the fact that I'd almost choked to death. "What do you think?''

"I think—" I stopped and thought about the left-over lasagna. "I think we'd better talk about this another time. I don't think I'm the best person to take this job on. Maybe you and Dave could tell Ma together."

Sophia frowned. "He wants to do it that way, but I'm afraid..." She hesitated.

I prodded her. "Afraid of what?"

She looked at me seriously, tears glistening in her eyes. "Afraid Ma will have a heart attack."

I wasn't sure what to say. What was Sophia thinking? That Ma won't have a heart attack if *I* tell her? Or maybe it would just sound better coming from the responsible daughter? The really weird thing about all of this is that Ma has always thought the world of her oldest daughter. Sophia could do no wrong, even when she got pregnant with Michael before marrying the father, even when Sophia and her old man got a divorce, even when Sophia took a job at a dive of a biker bar—as if there were any other type of biker bar. And Sophia was worried about what Ma thought.

Of course, this was different, even I had to admit that. Ma was a devout Catholic and she could forgive pregnancy out of wedlock (they eventually got married, didn't they?) and Sophia's job (Ma never went near Sophia's place of employment, so out of sight, out of mind, right?). And as far as the divorce, well, Ma had conveniently forgotten the marriage. I think if Sophia ever got married again, Ma would be delighted. Of course, Sophia wasn't a practicing Catholic, so a second marriage would be overlooked in Ma's eyes. But a married man? Ma might not be able to ignore the fact that both Sophia *and* her suitor were divorced if Dave went ahead with his divorce.

We talked a little longer, but neither of us came up with a satisfying solution. Soon she had to leave for work, and I returned to my third-floor apartment. I took a hot bath and was ready to turn in when the phone rang.

Before I even had a chance to say hello, the gravelly voice on the other end of the line announced herself. "It's me."

"Ma, what're you doin' calling me so late?" My kitchen clock's second hand was just a few minutes from striking ten. Ma usually was in bed by nine-thirty.

"I heard you needed a new answering machine, so I called Uncle Sol, who's manager of Buy-Mart on Washington near the Park Street station."

"Yeah?" I was pleased to hear this. "You must have talked to Rosa today."

"She called me while she was looking after Stephie and Mikey." Sophia's kids, Stephanie and Michael, had recently become Stephie and Mikey to Ma. I think she was tired of the formality of the names. "Anyway, Uncle Sol told me you should stop by his store tomorrow—lunchtime is best—and he'd give you a good deal on a machine."

"Thanks, Ma." She's my own personal discount catalogue.

"By the way, I hope you're still coming to dinner on Sunday."

"Don't I always?"

"Sophia's bringing her young man here. She told me you know him."

"Mmmm." I tried to be noncommittal. Ma was fishing for more on Dave. "Listen, Ma. I have to be up early. Talk to you later?"

We hung up, Ma probably slightly frustrated that I'd sidestepped giving her information about Dave.

The next day, Ev stopped by early in the morning and dropped off the records he promised me. I went over them carefully, which took me almost two hours. And it was worth it. Seems the private investigator he'd hired had been very thorough after all, and there were even a few leads that had petered out early in the investigation. I could see how frustrating it was for both Ev and John Patton, the PI from San Francisco that he'd hired.

For instance, Patton had discovered that Earlene and Edie had been back to see Earlene's family in Kentucky for a brief time, about a week, right after their disappearance. Leatherwood was a small town situated between the Cumberland Plateau and Pine Mountain. With a population under five hundred, it wasn't hard for Patton to find someone who was willing to talk. I was just glad it was he, and not me, who made the trip to Leatherwood to get one of Earlene's cousins to talk. Okay, so I'm only guessing it was a cousin. With a population that small, I'm positive everyone there is related in one way or the other.

Later that morning, I took the T to Government Center and began my search for Earlene and Edie by checking voter registration records at City Hall. I looked under Earlene Morrow, E. Morrow, Everett Morrow, Mrs. Everett Morrow, and under her maiden name, Earlene Whipple. Nothing. I hadn't expected anything; Earlene never struck me as the type of woman who gave a damn who was president, let alone who sat on her city council. But it never hurts to look.

At the motor vehicle department, I looked for a driver's license, but again came up blank. If she lived in the Boston area near a T station, she probably used public transportation. Driving around Boston is just an exercise in frustration if you're new to the area. And the likelihood that Earlene was using an alias added to my frustration.

I went through all the avenues at city hall, including the tax assessor's office, and had no luck. I skipped the county courthouse, deciding to save the marriage records as a last resort—Earlene and Edie had only been here a few months, not enough time for Earlene to find a man and marry him. Of course, from what I remembered of Earlene, anything was possible. Still, it was a better bet to check school records. I went to the Suffolk County Superintendent of Schools office and tried to get a handle on Earlene through Edie.

"What did you say her name was? Eden Whipple or Eden Morrow?" the woman behind the counter asked me. Her nameplate told me that her name was Mrs. H. Arbuckle. Honest to God, she had blue hair and rhinestone glasses. I thought I'd stepped into the '50s or '60s for a moment. But she was helpful. Unfortunately, not helpful enough.

"Sorry," Mrs. H. Arbuckle said with a shrug after delving into her computerized files. "If it's any consolation, it's possible that she is attending one of our schools but her records haven't been sent here yet.

We do get new students all the time, coming in half-way through a school year because their parents had to move here for a job or for the military. Sometimes it takes a couple of months to get the records through all that red tape.''

I thanked her and left. I was determined to continue the search, this time making an on-site check. The problem was that there were over fifty middle schools in Boston and surrounding areas. But I was certain that as bad a mother as Earlene was, she would still have to enroll her daughter in some school, if she was in this area. I took out the photo of Edie and decided to start hitting the schools themselves tomorrow.

The rest of the day was devoted to my other paying work. I had to give my report—Rosa's report—to my MassTix client. The offices were located on the corner of Tremont and Temple and was an easy walk for me through the Common, Boston's oldest park.

The Common was quite a sight in the fall. Itinerant musicians, performers, and drug dealers littered the area along Tremont Street, all trying to attract the tourist trade. There were a couple of musicians I enjoyed listening to when they visited Boston, and I was fortunate to find one of them seated by his guitar case, entertaining both tourists and locals alike. The drug dealers were rampant, and I did my best to avoid them. The police kept an eye on the Common and tried to keep it clean, but there were always a couple of dealers who slipped through the cracks.

Then I saw something that filled me with dread—it was worse than a drug dealer, it was a *mime!* They sense a victim more surely than a crack dealer—and they zero in on that discomfort with a vengeance. I think most mimes are unhappy people whose goal in life is to make others as miserable and uncomfortable as they are. Maybe it's all that makeup.

This particular mime's expression brightened when he saw my trepidation, and he made a beeline toward me. I groaned. If there was one law I wanted to see on the books, it was a law banning mimes. They reminded me of those little gnats that come out on summer nights by the river and swarm around your face. No matter how many times you swat at them, they keep coming back for more.

I could feel him behind me, mimicking my purposeful walk, smirking his rubber-face smirk, and I could hear the nervous laughs from tourists. Then I did what a pedestrian usually doesn't do: I stopped dead in my tracks, and the mime slammed into me. I quickly turned around, hoping a face-to-face confrontation would put him off. Unfortunately, that didn't stop him. He may have been startled for a second or so, but when he realized he was in for a staring contest with me, he recovered nicely and began aping my every little twitch and blink. After a few minutes, I realized that I was making an ass of myself and began calling up aikido's first rule: Avoid confrontational situations.

I wondered what my fellow aikidoists would think of what my Italian temper had gotten me into. What to do from here? I didn't have time to spend in a pointless staring contest, but how was I going to get out of this gracefully? All of a sudden, the mime's nose began to twitch.

"Ah-ah-ah-choo!"

Without thinking, I whipped a blue tissue out of my shoulder bag and rubbed the mime's nose. "Geshundheit," I replied.

The mime grabbed the tissue and stared at it. "You creep," he hissed, "you ruined my makeup job!"

Cackles came from the impromptu audience, as did a smattering of applause. The mime looked around sheepishly, then grabbed my wrist, trying to yank me down in a semblance of a bow. Without thinking, I stepped back, trapped his hand between my free hand and his grip on my wrist, and performed a *nikkyo* submission hold on him by bringing my free hand over his wrist and putting pressure on it by leaning slightly forward and down.

"Uh! What th—?" The mime dropped to his knees, his face contorted with surprise and pain. The tourists laughed and clapped with delight.

I let up on the hold and stepped back. The mime stood up and rubbed his wrist.

I smiled and shrugged. "Sorry about that. You caught me by surprise."

As I turned to go, I heard him mutter, "I caught *her* by surprise?"

I managed to drop off my report without seeing my client. He was out with one of *his* clients, and his secretary scheduled a meeting for us for the next morning.

The other thing I had to do was get an answering machine. Buy-Mart was about six blocks away, near the heart of Chinatown. Uncle Sol was on his lunch break.

Uncle Sol got up and pulled out a box. "This is it. I can let you have it for wholesale. User-friendly, it not only answers messages but lets you pick up messages from any phone. You can change your message even if you're in Los Angeles." I bought it on the spot.

I then spent the rest of the afternoon wrestling with installing the damn thing, cursing it with every breath in my body. But by four o'clock, I was proud to say that I had installed it, and it seemed to be working by the time Rosa breezed into the office.

"Where've you been?" I asked, being careful to keep the peevish tone out of my voice.

"Got a call from one of your insurance companies and thought I'd pick up the work for you." Rosa reached into the briefcase that was dangling from one hand and extended a sheaf of paperwork.

I paged through it, realizing that most of it was routine question-and-answer investigating. One case involved a little more—following a woman named Betty DaSilva who claimed that she had been on a city bus that had been rear-ended, and she now had a bad back. I decided Rosa could be promoted into solo fieldwork while I was following up on Ev's missing daughter. I explained the work to my sister, whose eyes sparkled at the thought of going solo.

"Now, don't get any ideas that this is glamorous work, Rosa," I warned her. "Remember our stakeout the other day."

"Don't worry, Sarge," Rosa said with a salute. "You can count on me."

I rolled my eyes and wondered what I'd gotten myself into.

SIX

THE NEXT DAY, after my meeting with my MassTix client in the early morning, I hoofed it around Boston, introducing myself to the secretaries at the main offices of the middle schools, explaining the heartbreaking details of my search for the missing girl.

It was hard to get the secretaries and principals to talk to me. They had either experienced parental abductions, or they had heard the horror stories from other school systems. Some of the school officials met my inquiries with suspicion, but most were sympathetic, although they couldn't tell me much due to school policy.

I suppose I could have staked out every school, two a day—one in the morning when the children went in and one in the afternoon when they left—until I found Edie, but that seemed to be the slow way to do it.

Since Earlene had been an alcoholic and a drug user, I briefly considered checking out the drug activity in each area, showing Earlene's photo to dealers. But then I got a brainstorm: I went directly to the schoolyards and waited for the kids who were skipping a class or two for a quick smoke. There were always a few kids who wanted to test the boundaries. I felt like some kind of pervert standing just inside the chain-link fence, showing Edie's photo to kids who were copping a quick smoke before the bell rang. Fortunately, middle schools include only three grades—seventh, eighth, and ninth—so it's like a small community. Most kids, even the disaffected who hung around the edge of the school boundaries, would remember the newcomers this year.

I had started at the heart of Boston with the Back Bay and fanned my way out. I wished it were an easy job, just pick up the phone and call around, but I needed to show the photo of Edie, get a response—gauge whether someone was telling me the truth or trying to protect the child because of some story that Earlene might have told them about Edie's father.

When I had eliminated the Boston schools, I started in on the suburbs around the Lechmere area of Somerville, then Cambridge, Belmont, and Watertown. By the time I got to Brookline and Newton, I figured I'd eliminated the west suburbs and could start with the north of Boston. It was getting close to three-thirty—about the time the schools let out—and I called it a day. I figured I could start on Malden, Everett, Chelsea, and Revere tomorrow.

When I got back to my place, I was ready for a nice glass of red wine and some baked ziti. I'd fixed Ma's famous sauce and frozen the leftovers a couple of weeks ago, and it wouldn't do to leave it sitting in my freezer when I had an urge for ziti. The recipe for the sauce has been handed down in Ma's family for generations. Along with the pork chops, Italian sausage (I like it hot), and meatballs, the secret is to throw a couple of chicken legs in, and then simmer the sauce for three to four hours.

I had just put a pot of water on to boil for the spaghetti when I heard whispering coming from my bedroom. I turned off the gas under the pot and grabbed the marble rolling pin off the counter, then crept toward the slightly open door. Rustling sounds sent chills up my back, and I thought I heard the urgent whispers of at least two people. I wished I had my gun, but I'd left it locked in the bottom drawer of my desk back in my office, the way all good detectives do.

The rolling pin was getting heavy, and the handle was small and unwieldy. I tried to imagine swinging it over my head, the marble breaking off and whacking *me* on the noggin. I tossed the rolling pin on my sofa and decided to take my chances. After all, I *had* been taking aikido.

Kicking the door open, I leaped in, ready to take on all comers. The comers were Sophia and David— in my bed. I shrieked. David had the sense to pull on a pair of pants, but Sophia lolled around on my bed, the sheets up around her armpits, smiling like the cat who snagged the chicken off of my plate on Ma's dining room table.

"What the fuck are you doing here?" I asked, directing my wrath at Sophia.

She smiled calmly. "Michael and Stephanie are doing their homework in my apartment, and we needed someplace to meet. I happened to have a copy of your key."

"Which you must have copied at some point when I wasn't aware of it." I could feel the steam coming out of my ears. I still hadn't looked at David directly, but out of the corner of my eye, I could see he had that wounded puppy look to him.

Sophia threw the covers off and stood up, completely in the altogether. "Oh, for God's sake," I managed to sputter before grabbing my white terry-cloth robe and tossing it to her.

While ogling my sister, David managed to get his shirt on and give me a weak apology. "Uh, Angie, I'm really sorry about all of this. I meant to tell you…"

I sighed and crossed my arms. "Meant to tell me what, David? That you and Sophia have been having this hot and heavy affair for the past several months? That's not news. What I don't understand is why here? Why my place? Why without asking?"

David seemed at a loss, but, as usual, Sophia made up for it. "Don't be stupid, Angie. We couldn't possibly do the wild thing with the children in the apartment." My sister, the prude. Yeesh.

"Oh, of course, how silly of me." I threw my hands up and walked back into the living room. David followed me, but when I tried to make eye contact with him, he avoided my direct gaze, his face slightly flushed.

We stood around in uncomfortable silence for a few minutes, long enough for both of us to imagine near future encounters at the dojo, until Sophia emerged from the bedroom. She looked dewy fresh and unruffled in an off-the-shoulder white peasant blouse and a three-tiered print skirt. I wanted to smack her. Instead, I held out my hand. She looked at it flatly.

"The key," I explained, trying to prompt her elusive memory.

She dug into the pocket of her skirt and handed it to me. The image of a drawer full of these keys in

Sophia's ground-floor apartment flashed through my mind, but I tried to wave it off.

Dave glanced surreptitiously at Sophia, and she returned his glance with a fond smile. "Maybe I shouldn't go to Sunday dinner," he said hesitantly.

Sophia touched his cheek gently. It was really weird to see my sister, the one who always brought home tattooed, leather-jacketed boyfriends, looking so much in love. "Don't be like that. Ma's anxious to meet you."

Because she doesn't know you're married, I finished silently.

Dave started out the door. I wanted to say something to him, but the look he'd given me earlier made me wonder if he was mad at me, or if he was just embarrassed by being caught in flagrante delicto. I decided not to say anything inflammatory. "See you later, Dave."

Dave paused and, without turning around to look at me, said, "Yeah. See you, Angie."

Sophia started to go with him. I caught her by the arm and hissed, "I want to talk to you. Now."

She narrowed her eyes, but nodded shortly. "I'll see you to the door, Dave. Angie and I are going to discuss next Sunday at Ma's." Oh, that sisterly connection. Without even a small hint, Sophia had picked up exactly what I wanted to talk about.

She came back a minute later, her cheeks flushed. "He's so nice, Angie. I think I could fall in love with him."

I'd never seen her act like this with any of the losers she usually went out with. I almost regretted my next words. "Are you insane?"

Sophia whirled around, crossing her arms petu-
lantly, her skirt swirling out in an appealing manner,
her dark hair fanning out around her shoulders. "You
don't like seeing me happy?"

I finally uprooted my feet and moved around to
talk to her face. "No, I mean, yes, it's great that
you're happy, and Dave's a great guy, but he's still
a great *married* guy."

She looked up at me with a sly expression. "Separated, Angie. He's separated."

"Separated isn't the same as single. Or divorced.
Or widowed. Or annulled." I tried to think of other
examples of alternative singlehood, and only gay
came to mind, but I didn't think it was relevant to
the situation, so I abandoned it. "Anyway, that's not
the point I was going to make. If you want to see a
separated guy, that's none of my business. What is
my business is that you want to bring him home to
Ma and pass him off as single." I paused dramatically. "I'm not going to be the one who tells her.
You and Dave have to figure this out for yourselves."

"It hasn't come up yet. When Ma invited Dave
along, she assumed that he's single," Sophia reluctantly admitted. "I just haven't found the right time
to tell her. She'll get along great with him." A smile
lit up her face. I swear I've never seen her so happy,
so... in love.

"When do you plan to break the news to her?" I
asked. "She hasn't even met him yet, but you know
she's already planning the wedding. Stephanie as
flower girl and Michael as ring bearer."

"Michael's too old to be a ring bearer," Sophia

said absently. "I suppose one of our brothers could supply us with a youngster from their litters of kids."

My three brothers were all married, two of them happily. They all had between three and five kids each. It's gotten so I can't remember names or ages anymore, and I end up getting reminder calls from my sisters-in-law whenever a niece or nephew's birthday is close, which seems to be about once a week these days. I figured that when Rosa and I ended up having kids, our siblings would owe those kids big time in the gift department.

"It almost sounds like you're planning the frigging wedding yourself," I snapped.

Sophia blinked rapidly for a moment as if she were waking up from some lovely dream. Her brow furrowed. "You're right, Ange. But what's done is done."

"What if Ma starts asking me questions about Dave?" I pointed out. "What then? What'm I supposed to tell her?"

Sophia's eyes widened, a spark of panic in them. "I don't know. You'll think of something."

I could see where this was heading. Big sister Sophia had it bad. "You're thinking he might file for divorce between now and when you tell her?" I smiled cynically. "Don't count on it, sweetie."

There didn't seem to be much more to say, and true to the formula of most Matelli arguments, the subject was dropped cold so that Sophia could bring Stephanie and Michael up to my place for the evening. Before Sophia went to work, I picked up where I left off with making dinner, and we all sat around to a big batch of baked ziti.

After Sophia took off for work, I kept the kids entertained with my new Sega Genesis system while I waited for Rosa to come home. About nine-thirty, the downstairs door slammed shut and Rosa's footsteps on the stairs prompted me to run into the hall and call down.

"Hey, Rosa, come on up!" There was a pause, then her light tread on the stairs as she jogged up to my place. She had a sheaf of papers in one hand and her eyes sparkled as she began telling me about her day.

"Oh, Sarge! You wouldn't believe the day I had," she said. "First, I got through the routine insurance investigations pretty quick. I'd say by eleven they were done."

I paged through the documents, noting that she had been very thorough in her analysis of the cases. I was impressed.

"And what did you do the rest of the day?" I asked.

Before she could answer, the two youngsters came hurtling into Rosa's arms from the other room.

"Hi, Aunt Rosa!" Stephanie and Michael yelled in unison.

"Come play Mortal Kombat with us!" Michael demanded.

"Michael cheats," Stephanie said, her hands on her hips and a dangerous glint in her eye.

"Do not!"

"Do, too!"

I stepped in between them. "Aunt Rosa and I have to talk. You two will just have to work it out yourselves." I steered the gruesome twosome back toward the soft glow of the beckoning television; then Rosa and I went into the kitchen.

"And clean up the blood when you're done!" I yelled to my little charges before grabbing a brew out of the refrigerator and popping the top. Rosa helped herself to a wine cooler. We sat at Ma's old chrome and mottled-gray formica dinette table. The chairs were a snazzy gray-and-red plastic. I was beginning to like fifties stuff and was thinking of decorating the rest of my place in that style. It would be cheaper to furnish if I stuck to yard sales and second-hand joints here in East Boston.

Rosa told me that she'd had an afternoon appointment with the university bursar's office to go over her status.

"I told them I was taking some time off to decide what I wanted to major in," she recounted sheepishly.

I nodded approvingly. "Good idea. Don't make any big decisions about your situation until you decide what's right for you."

"And tomorrow, I'll start surveillance on Betty DaSilva, that woman with the bad back."

"Take the briefcase with the video camera in it," I instructed her. "You know how to use it?"

Rosa nodded. "I watched you."

"Make sure there's tape in it," I said with a grin.

Rosa wrinkled her nose at me. Then it was my turn. I recounted my earlier adventure with Sophia and Dave for my sister's benefit, enjoying watching her take a swig from her wine cooler, then roll her eyes dramatically at the right parts.

When I was finished, she shook her head. "Boy, Sarge, I'm not sure what I would have done."

I grinned. "You would've probably apologized for interrupting them and gently closed the door on your way out."

She wrinkled her nose. "Am I that bad?"

"No, you're that nice, Rosa. Sometimes I think you were a changeling. You don't have that hot Italian temper like the rest of us."

By the time we finished our drinks, I was getting sleepy from my big, emotion-filled day. Michael and Stephanie were ready to stay up all night, and it took about half an hour to calm them down. We finally separated them—Rosa taking Michael down to her spare bedroom while I wrestled with Stephanie to get her to brush her teeth and put on her pajamas. Since Sophia worked until two in the morning or sometimes later, we had an agreement that the kids stayed with Rosa and me on their mother's work nights.

When I finally got Stephanie settled down in my guest room, I tried to get some sleep of my own. But thoughts of Edie, the missing girl, kept intruding, keeping me awake as I anticipated continuing the investigation tomorrow.

SEVEN

BEFORE I LEFT THE OFFICE the next morning, I got a call from Ev. "Just wondering if you have anything to report."

I paused, wondering how to make my totally useless day sound good. "Well, I eliminated Boston and the immediate area to the west—Brookline, Cambridge, Newton, Belmont, Watertown, and Somerville."

"Don't know the area too well. Doesn't mean a thing to me," Ev replied. "But I bet it means that you didn't find out anything yet."

"Nothing concrete," I admitted. "But elimination is the name of the game. You should know that."

He sighed audibly over the phone line. "Yeah, Matelli, I know that." He hadn't called me Matelli since our marine days. It gave me a warm feeling all over, followed by a slow shudder.

"I'm hitting the suburbs today north of Lechmere."

"How are you going about your search?"

I winced, then decided to go for a light tone. "If I told you, Ev, you might not want to keep me on retainer."

"Come on, Matelli, give," he growled.

I assured him that I would have something for him by the end of the week. I wished I felt as confident as I sounded.

I worked the north suburbs of Boston, finally hitting pay dirt in Revere at about one in the afternoon. I couldn't tell whether the kid I met with was a boy or a girl. Grungy, long, drab-brown hair, flannel plaid shirt over a well-worn (and infrequently washed) gray T-shirt and baggy Army pants was the style of the day. The acne-scarred face looked up at me through sleepy lids.

"Excuse me, can you help me with some information?"

"Depends," it said. I took a wild guess and decided it could be a boy.

I took Edie's dog-eared photo out of my pocket and showed it to him. "Do you know this girl? Does she go to school here?"

He took a long look, shrugged, and lit a cigarette. "She might. What's it to you?"

"What's your name?" I asked, trying to sound official.

He eyed me for a moment while weighing his answer. "Weezer. After the band—you know?" His expression told me he doubted I did. He sucked on his Marlboro and let a stream of smoke swirl into the warm spring air.

I took a moment to assess whom I was dealing with. Weezer was probably bored with school. He probably didn't give a damn about Edie. Maybe I could liven it up for him.

"Okay... Weezer. I'm going to level with you." I took out a fake badge and flipped it at him, hoping he wasn't into clamming up on the establishment. Sure enough, his eyes widened imperceptibly. He was still trying to maintain his cool, but I could tell he was impressed.

"FBI," I said crisply. "We would appreciate your cooperation." Always use the universal "we" when talking to a witness—one of the first lessons I learned in the Criminal Investigations Division of the Military Police. People are more impressed by a phantom "we" than a tangible "I." It sounds more official, I guess.

I edged closer to him, looking around as if there were electronic bugs everywhere. "We're trying to locate Edie's mother."

Weezer's eyes were already pretty wide. They widened even further. "Drugs?"

"Mmmm," I murmured in a noncommittal tone. "Edie could be in danger. You'd be a big help if—"

"I've seen a girl who looks like her," Weezer said eagerly, flicking his cigarette butt into the street. "I think it's the same girl. I don't know her name, but I always notice the new students. I think she's in seventh grade."

I nodded and extracted a promise from Weezer that at three o'clock, he'd be out front to point her out. The ten I gave him helped. We agreed that he couldn't be seen with me—more for his reputation as a malcontent than my reputation as a nonexistent agent for the FBI—but I'd watch him, and when he lit up a Marlboro, I'd know Edie was coming out the front door. It was a little convoluted, but for the sake of appearances, and because I was adding a little excitement to his life, I agreed.

I killed time by driving to Revere Beach to watch the ocean. It had always been a peaceful experience when I came here. There really isn't much of a place to walk on the beach, but you can walk along a seawall while the waves try to climb up over it. There's nothing quite like it, in my opinion—witnessing the ocean beat itself against the Revere Beach wall.

But today, I didn't find that peace. I thought back to that article in the *Globe* about the body that had been found here, that of a young girl about Edie's age. I shuddered and quickened my pace, anxious to get back to the school.

I was back by three and standing in my designated area. I caught sight of Weezer by the big double doors of the school, attempting to look natural, probably having second thoughts about squealing on a kid he didn't know anything about. He shifted from one foot to the other, the ten dollars I gave him earlier probably burning a hole in his pocket right now. Students started to come out in a wave, like the waves at Revere Beach but without the wall. The kids chattered, the sound rising and falling like crickets on an otherwise quiet night in the country.

Weezer never had a chance to flick his Bic. By the time the last kid came out, we were the only two standing there. He caught my eye and with a furtive movement of his head, indicated that I was to follow him at a distance. We met across the street behind a tree after he made sure no one could see him with me.

"I didn't see her. Maybe she's out sick today," he said.

I narrowed my eyes. "Are you sure you're telling me the truth?" I asked more harshly than I should have. "This isn't just some game you're playing, is it?"

"Hell, no," he said, his hands gesturing that I was all wrong. "I asked around and was told her name was Eden Morris. She hasn't been in school this week."

Morris is close enough to Morrow. It made sense. "A week? That's a long time."

He slipped a piece a paper in my hand, looking around in a furtive manner as he did so. "I did get her address for you." We could have skipped the James Bond routine if he'd just given it to me in the first place. I gave him another ten before walking away.

I hesitated about going to the house without finding out more information about Edie's attendance at school. I walked inside and looked around for the main office.

"Can I help you?" I turned to find a small, birdlike woman standing with her head cocked to one side.

"Um, I hope so. I'm looking for a student, Eden Morris." I shifted from one foot to the other, hoping this woman wasn't going to send for security to throw me out. I waited for the suspicious look to cross her face, but instead she looked vaguely worried. "Edie's one of my pupils. Yes, I'm worried about her, too. She hasn't been to school this week." The teacher extended a hand. "I'm Rita Power. You must be with the head office."

I smiled and gave a noncommittal nod. So far today, I could have been arrested for impersonating two officials. As long as I was on a roll...

"We're checking up on students who have been out of school for a week or more."

Ms. Power nodded, walking me slowly toward the main office. "I understand. But perhaps her absence can be explained. Her best friend recently died."

I pulled up short, suddenly seeing a whole new side to Edie. Of course she would have a best friend. I recalled the Edie I had known years ago—a bright seven-year-old, quiet, shy. She had scared me sometimes, she was so much like a miniature adult. Of course, I understood that often happened to the children of alcoholics—they became the parental figures. I could almost hear my heart breaking as I thought of what Edie's last six months had been like without the stable influence of her father.

"Her best friend was... ?"

Ms. Power blinked as if she couldn't believe I didn't know; then she looked away and sighed. "Yes, of course you wouldn't put it together. Rachel McCarthy, the little girl whose body was found washed up on Revere Beach early Monday morning. The memorial service was held this past weekend."

I nodded slowly, the information sinking in, forcing my heart to settle in my stomach. "Yes, of course. How tragic." Rosa had shown me the article when we were staking out the MassTix office.

Ms. Power pressed her lips together into a thin line, crossing her arms for emphasis. "I hope they find the killer. She didn't just drown, you know. The police have been here, asking around. We've had to bring counselors in to talk to some of the kids."

I was bothered by something Ms. Power had said earlier. "You mentioned that Edie hasn't been to class all week, yet Rachel McCarthy's body was found just two days ago.''

The teacher frowned, suddenly looking at me with a little suspicion. "You should have it in your records. Rachel's parents filed a missing child report as soon as they realized she wasn't coming back from school last Friday."

I nodded quickly. "Yes, I do have that information, but I didn't realize it had any bearing on Edie Morris's absence until now."

Ms. Power got a faraway look in her eyes, her fingers touching her chin. "I suppose that could be the case," she said slowly, softly. "I guess I just didn't put it together."

"What about Edie's folks? Have you heard from them?"

"Oh, Edie only has her mom. I just met with Mrs. Morris once," Ms. Power said, wrinkling her nose in distaste. "She gave me the impression that she was a widow."

She *would,* I thought as I confirmed the address with the teacher. I thanked her for her help, then left the building before Ms. Power had a chance to think about my questions too carefully.

EIGHT

It was a shabby little dwelling, hardly worthy of the title "house," on a small street called Shawmut by the railroad tracks. Wonderland Park was nearby, a deteriorated amusement park that now housed a dog track. It attracted a really classy sort of person, the kind who hangs around and brings down the property value without any effort at all.

I noticed a motorcycle parked on the lawn next to a couple of scattered and broken bikes. I walked up to the door and knocked. A nearby window was half open and I could hear movement inside, but no one answered. I raised my hand to knock again, and the door was yanked open. A tall, emaciated man with a mustache that attempted to hide his angry red acne scars brushed by me, almost knocking me down in the process. He wore a beat-up leather motorcycle jacket in the warm weather, which I thought was strange. Even the Hell's Angels Sophia had gone out with haven't been that addicted to their leather jackets.

A moment later, he climbed on his motorcycle, gave the house his middle finger, and yelled "Bitch!" I noted the license plate number before he roared off in a cloud of blue smoke.

I stuck my head in the doorway to call out. The first thing that hit me was the smell—a musty, moldy mixture of sweat, red wine, vomit, marijuana, and something I couldn't identify, but it smelled familiar. I soon found out what it was.

A woman was moaning. Remembering the angry look on the face of the man who bumped into me on his way out, I slipped inside, thinking someone was in trouble. I had to let my eyes adjust to the dimness. A television was going full blast in the living room, and several children were intently watching the Power Rangers fight some villain in a stupid-looking costume.

Across the room, my eyes encountered a large thrashing thing that I first thought was a black Labrador and an Irish setter playfully wrestling on the couch. But when the two dogs began growling things like, "Go, baby, go. Yeah, that's how I like it, baby, do it to me," I realized that it was a man with a hairy back and a red-haired woman having sex in front of the children. Well, technically, the children had their backs to the adults, but it was in the same room. Why was it my lot to walk in on two coital encounters in two days? Was someone up there trying to tell me something?

I wasn't sure whether to avert my eyes and blush, go over and throw cold water on them and explain to them why they need the privacy of a bedroom, or throw up. The unidentified smell was sex.

"Uh, hello?" I said tentatively. No one moved. All three kids were under five years old—one sucked his thumb, another held onto an old, hairless Barbie doll, and the third rocked back and forth, cradling a ratty-looking blanket. Their eyes never strayed from the screen.

If I'd been a social worker, those kids would have

been out of there as soon as possible—in, oh, say, five years. Nowadays, it seemed to take a lot to terminate someone's parental rights.

Before I could say or do anything else, the man and woman stopped what they were doing. I stepped back into the doorway, out of their field of vision. "Honey," the woman said, "I thought I heard somethin'. Let me check on the kids."

"Oh, baby," the man responded in a husky tone, "them kids is all right. It was just the TV. Let's move into the bedroom. Besides, Em'll watch the kids."

There were some kissing sounds as he convinced her to leave the kids alone and concentrate on him, then the sound of a door shutting firmly, followed by rhythmically squeaking bed springs.

I looked over at the kids, who hadn't moved a muscle. I cleared my throat. One of the kids slowly looked around at me. I moved forward. The girl didn't seem to be frightened, acting more like she was resigned to her fate, to whatever happened. I felt a chill run down my spine.

"Hello," I said in as nonthreatening a manner as I could, "can you tell me if Edie Morris lives here?"

The girl stared at me mutely. "She don't speak much," one of the boys told me. He was older than I'd originally estimated, maybe seven years old, but he held on to that blanket as if it were his lifeline.

He continued as if I wasn't staring dumbly at this pathetic excuse for child-rearing. "I haven't seen Edie in a while. But her mom's here." He got up, his eyes still glued to the brightly costumed superheroes and pointed down the hall to the first door.

"That's her room." Then he was back in front of the TV as if strange women always walked uninvited into his house.

I looked at the closed door and started to knock, but hesitated. Maybe it would be a good idea to find Edie's room first and see if there were any clues. I poked around until I found a room that was about the size of a school janitorial closet. But it had things that only a fourteen-year-old girl would own—posters of Boyz II Men and Janet Jackson, a couple of stuffed toys, a pink jewelry box that held cheap earrings, bracelets, and a ruby birthstone necklace. A Gameboy sat unused at the foot of the bed, several games scattered around it. A tape deck and several tapes sat on a cheap secondhand desk, along with schoolbooks for algebra, history, and government. An open notebook lay to one side of the desk, with hearts and flowers doodled in the margins. I flipped through it, noting the As and Bs she'd gotten on diagramming sentences and a pop quiz in biology.

It was a spartan room for a teenager, but then, Earlene was probably working at some menial job, and there probably wasn't a whole lot of money left over after paying for rent, utilities, groceries, alcohol, and drugs. I looked in the drawers, hoping to find a clue. I felt a little guilty that I was here before the police—but Ev was my client, Edie was his daughter, and I was just doing my job. If I found anything, I'd turn it over to whoever ended up with this case.

It was under her mattress, always a good place for a diary. I sat on the edge of her foam mattress bed and turned the pages, reading the secret thoughts and feelings of a stranded teen.

Sept. 5: I miss Daddy. When I ask Mom where he is, she just gets mad. Then she goes off and drinks. She says terrible things about him. I was mad at him for the first few weeks, mad that he didn't say goodbye, mad that he left me with Mom, and mad that I hadn't gotten a letter or call from him. I miss him so much. Whenever I ask about why we changed our last name, Mom just tells me that it has something to do with what Daddy does. It's to protect us. But I've known for some time that Mom needs me more than Daddy does. I just wish she'd let me talk to Daddy.

Sept. 15: Lately, I've been thinking Mom is making up stuff. I even thought about calling my old phone number, just to see if Mom was telling the truth. She's so screwed up. Sometimes I think she needs me more than I need her. I'd rather live in a foster home than here some days.

Sept. 16: I did it. I called the old number today when we were shopping at Lechmere. But I spotted Mom coming toward me and I hung up quick. It sounded like someone answered, but I couldn't tell who it was. I wish I'd stayed on the line. Even with Mom there. I hate it here.

Sept. 27: I've thought about what to do. Do I tell an adult? Adults screw things up so bad sometimes, I'm afraid to say anything. Life might get worse instead of better. Should I call the number again and see if someone answers? I could do it at Rachel's house. I've thought about talking to Rachel's parents, but I'm not sure they'd understand.

Sept. 29: I've decided that I have to do something. I don't want to live here anymore. I want to go home with Daddy. I don't believe Mom. I think Daddy's still around and he doesn't know where I am. Mom has been mad at him for years. She talks to me about what a bad husband he was, a bad father. But the things she says don't make sense to me. I've talked to Rachel about it, and she agreed to help me.

That was the last entry in her diary. So Rachel McCarthy had been recruited to help Edie—but how? I stuck the diary in my purse and left Edie's room.

I went back to Earlene's room and knocked, then opened the door, my eyes closed, hoping I wouldn't be treated to another coital encounter. "Hello?" I called out.

"Who the hell're you?"

I opened one eye, then the other. The blue haze of smoke made it difficult to see, but I could make out a figure on the mattress on the floor. She looked similar to the Earlene of my younger days, but she was unkempt, blowsy. Her face was pale and puffed out, reminding me of an older Shelley Winters, and she was holding a bottle of cheap wine, squeezing the neck of the bottle as if she were throttling it. Earlene squinted across the room at me. "You look familiar. You from my daughter's school?"

"No, Earlene, I'm not." I took the opportunity to

step inside and close the door. "I'm Angela Matelli. I used to know you when you were married to Ev."

"Matelli," she said my last name dreamily, "I remember you. You're the slut who stole my man."

I sighed, not even tempted to get angry. It was too sad. "Earlene, I transferred out of Ev's command over seven years ago."

"You were all alike, all the women Ev slept with. He always denied it, but I knew he was steppin' out on me." She eyed me for a moment, then, having apparently decided to forego the amenity of a glass, took a slug of wine. Some of it dribbled down her cheek, staining her cheap Japanese-print robe.

What was the point of denying an affair with Ev? It was clear that Earlene would believe what she wanted to believe. Nothing I said would change that. "I'm not here about Ev. I'm here about Edie."

She wiped her face with the sleeve of her robe. "What, you want to take her away from me, too?"

What was with this woman? It was all I could do to maintain my calm. I decided to dispense with formalities like explaining my interest in Edie. Earlene was way into the self-pity mode of drinking and hadn't thought through the reason for my being there.

"The school hasn't seen her in a week. What about you? Have you seen her lately?" I couldn't believe I was asking this question of a parent. But I didn't regard Earlene as a parent, more like a child in an adult's body who couldn't comprehend the concept of responsibility.

Earlene stood up, a little unsteady on her pins. "Say, what're you doin' here?" Her eyes narrowed.

"This wouldn't have anything to do with Ev, would it?"

I had to give her credit—she was quick. I'd been there a whole five minutes, and it had only taken her this long to figure out that my appearance wasn't random.

I sighed impatiently. "Ev hired me to find Edie. Have you seen her lately?"

Earlene's eyes narrowed in her puffy face. "Why you?"

"I live in Boston and I'm a private investigator. Where's Edie?"

Earlene—big surprise—ignored the question yet again. "You're screwin' him. I know it. That's why he sent you here." She came at me, brandishing her wine bottle. The woman had a one-track mind and, pathetic as it was, I was fed up.

I met her head on and grabbed handfuls of her cheap robe, pushing her up against a wall. The bottle fell away with a thud and I heard the glug, glug, glug of wine seeping out of it.

"I'm not here to fight over Ev like a couple of schoolgirls," I said in a low voice.

Earlene's eyes widened. I let go of her and backed away. She crossed the room and sat back on the bed.

"You should be concerned about Edie, for God's sake, not who your ex is screwing. Edie's missing, isn't she?"

When Earlene spoke, it was in the timid Kentucky-born accent I remembered from seven years ago. "Ev doesn't have her? I thought she went back to him." She looked away.

"Ev has spent three months searching for her," I replied in an even voice.

Earlene's expression was bitter. "Ev can go to hell, for all I care."

"At least Ev didn't lie to Edie about her mother."

Earlene paled. "What're you talking about?"

"You lied to Edie to get her to go with you, didn't you?" I got nasty. "Did you let her think that something awful had happened to her father and that she would never see him again? Is that the only way you thought you could keep your daughter?"

Her face screwed up, on the verge of either crying or bursting with rage. "What the hell would you know about kids? You don't know what it's like to be a parent. You're probably a dyke, anyway."

Oh, so now that I've made it clear that her ex and I didn't sleep together, now I'm a lesbian. I smiled, trying to maintain a cool exterior. "Name-calling isn't going to help your daughter," I pointed out. "Edie called Ev from the Lechmere area of Somerville about a week ago, and he hired me to continue the search. How long has she been gone?"

The rage seemed to drain from her as quickly as it began. Her voice was little more than a whisper. "I-I don't know."

"So you figured she'd gone back to Ev."

She sank down to her haunches like some wild animal. "Yes." She looked up at me with frightened, beady eyes and cringed.

My hands were clenched and I kept my arms rigid at my sides so I wouldn't be tempted to punch her lights out. "And you didn't check?"

Earlene turned her bitter gaze to a worn Peter Max

poster nearby. "All she ever did was talk about Ev. I knew she'd leave eventually." She stood up and walked unsteadily over to the dresser, taking a pack of generic cigarettes and a Bic lighter from a drawer. "Edie might have figured out where to contact Ev. When she didn't come home Friday afternoon, I knew she was going back to Ev."

"But she didn't," I pointed out, trying to keep myself in check. "She's a minor who's been missing for almost a week."

Earlene paused to light her cigarette and inhale. As she blew smoke out of her nostrils—a particularly unpleasant habit, in my opinion—she shrugged and wrapped her arms around her thin waist. "I guess I never was much of a mother."

"Who was the guy who left here a few minutes ago?"

She looked bewildered. I described him. Her face cleared, which was more than I could say for the biker's face. "Oh, that's Stick."

"Did he know Edie?"

She nodded, distracted now by her fallen bottle of wine. After picking it up and downing the remaining, she added, "He wouldn't know nothin' 'bout Edie runnin' away." Earlene stopped, narrowed her eyes, and stared at me. She took a pill bottle out of her robe pocket and fiddled with it.

"He seemed mad about something," I said.

She dropped her eyes to the bottle and mumbled, "We just had a fight is all. He'll be back." Something about the way she said it and her smug smile made me a little queasy.

I was getting nowhere fast. I tried another avenue. "Did you know her best friend, Rachel McCarthy?"

"I don't even know why I'm still talkin' to you," she replied. She crossed the room and sat down on her bed again. "But, yeah, I knew Rachel. Nice kid. Edie was ashamed of me, of our living situation. But she did bring Rachel home a couple of times. Once to sleep over."

My shoulders sagged. I felt a little sick. "Then I guess you don't read the papers too often."

Earlene cocked her head and frowned, squinting from the drifting cigarette smoke. "What you talkin' about?"

"Rachel's body was found along Revere Beach early Monday morning."

Earlene dropped our eye contact, suddenly gazing at the floor. She squeezed her eyes shut for a moment and scrunched her face up as if she were in pain. "That don't mean a thing, does it? Edie wasn't found with Rachel, was she? I mean, Edie could still be around, maybe just hiding, couldn't she? Edie's alright, isn't she?"

"Is she?" I gave Earlene a cool appraisal. I didn't think that she was smart enough to hide Edie, but it had been known to happen. I took a step toward her. "Earlene—"

Earlene held up her hands defensively, still not looking at me. She gave a caustic little laugh. "I guess I was right when I said I wasn't much of a mother."

NINE

I LEFT THE HOUSE only after obtaining the name of Earlene's roommate, who was nowhere to be found when we went looking for her and her lover.

"Bobbie must've gone off to work," Earlene had explained. "And her boyfriend, Herb, has gone back to his wife."

I winced. A married lover would prove difficult to interview, unless I could catch him at work. I felt like I was stuck in the middle of a C&W song. Earlene gave me the addresses and phone numbers of Herb and Bobbie's former lover, Joe Blount, who had been unceremoniously dumped the night of Edie's disappearance.

In fact, Earlene was so free and easy with her roommate's name and other information that it was hard to believe how difficult it was to obtain information from her about her own life. But then, Earlene had been living on the run for the last few months, and she had never struck me as a honest person in the first place. Still, it was obvious to me that she was being evasive when I asked her about Stick. I shrugged it off, knowing that I'd just have to find out about him the hard way.

She had appeared to be cooperative once it sank in that her daughter was missing, but I couldn't be sure if her concern was for herself. She could be charged by the state with child neglect and endangerment and any number of other charges that the State Attorney could dredge up. Or did she truly care about Edie?

I hoped it was the latter. Earlene was an alcoholic, a drug addict—I'd seen the mirrors and the white powder residue on her dresser—and might want to get back at her ex-husband, but she had to have some feelings for the child or she wouldn't have kept Edie with her all this time. She would have left her back in Kentucky with her relatives.

Just before I went home, I had the contents of the diary copied. I would have to turn the original over to the cops, but there was no law saying I couldn't have a copy of it. Although I'm pretty sure there's a law against taking it in the first place.

It was almost six o'clock when I got home. I called into my office for my messages, using my personal code to listen to them. There was a message from Ev, and another from Ma. Of course. I called Ev and gave him my report, including the possible connection between Rachel McCarthy and his daughter.

"Edie's been missing since Friday and Earlene's not worried?" Ev's usually reserved manner was gone. His little girl had gone missing twice now, and the second time around involved her murdered best friend. "Damn it, Angie, give me Earlene's address. She's lying. I'll get the truth from her."

I was glad that I hadn't given Earlene's address to him yet. We didn't need another murder. "Ev, calm down. I think it would be a mistake for you to confront Earlene right now."

"A mistake! Edie's disappeared and my ex is in an alcoholic fog. The mistake will be yours if you don't let me get the truth out of her.'' His voice was tight with anger and desperation.

"Ev, you hired me to look for Edie and I'm still doing that. And whatever you may think of your ex-wife, she seems to be sincere in her concern for Edie's disappearance.'' The concern may be for herself, of course, but I didn't think it needed to be said aloud. "I've got it from several reliable sources that Edie's been out of school all week, about the same amount of time as the McCarthy girl. We'll talk about a meeting with Earlene when you've calmed down,'' I said, adding, "and you won't see her alone. I'll go with you.''

I convinced him that the next step was to file a missing persons report with the police. We agreed to meet at the Revere police station in an hour.

I had just hung up when the phone rang.

"Sarge?'' the timid voice sounded tinny over the telephone wire. It was Rosa, who was supposed to be working on the insurance fraud case, keeping surveillance on the woman with the bad back.

"Rosa? Where are you?''

"Sarge, I'm in jail. This is my one phone call.''

"Oh, God, Rosa!'' I slapped the side of my face, which tingled, and closed my eyes. "What happened?''

"Well, uh, you see, I was following that woman, you see, and—'' Rosa paused, then burst out with, "Sarge, I was arrested for loitering.''

"How the hell did you do that?'' I didn't have time for the full story and it sounded as if I wasn't going to get it until I saw Rosa that night. I had a meeting with Ev in half an hour. "Look, Rosa. Can you hang on there for about an hour and a half?"

"I don't know, Sarge; some of the women here in my holding cell are a little rough." I tried to picture my little sister trying to find common ground with ladies of the evening, or maybe worse. Was it my imagination or was Rosa's voice a little shaky? "Uh, Sarge? One of the women propositioned me."

Uh-oh. I had to meet Ev, but my little sister was in trouble. I couldn't be in two places at once. I had an idea. "What station are you at?"

"Berkeley," she said shortly.

I told her to hang in there and promised her that she would be out soon. Then I called Lee Randolph, my police detective friend and fellow ex-marine. I hoped he was still working the night shift.

Lee answered, and I breathed a sigh of relief. "What's up, Angie? You're not looking for that poker money I owe you, are you?"

I'd met Lee during my first case, and we'd formed a bond based on our military backgrounds. I wish I was interested in him as more than a friend, but we'd already had "the Talk." You know, the "I-like-you-a-lot-but-only-as-a-friend" talk. Still, we went out occasionally, and a couple Fridays a month we played poker with a bunch of guys. Lee was about the worst player I'd ever seen.

"No, I wouldn't call you on duty to hassle you about that," I said, then launched into an explanation of Rosa's situation. When he stopped laughing, he promised that he'd talk with someone downstairs and straighten the whole thing out. Rosa would be out of the pokey before long. "But I can't promise that she's off the hook entirely. She may still have to appear in court.''

"Thanks, Lee.'' I paused and had another thought. "By the way, do you happen to know anyone who works for the Revere police?''

"Yeah, a guy named Ted MacMillan. He just transferred from Vice to Homicide. Why do you want to know?''

I briefly outlined my case, not giving him all the details, just the bare facts. I didn't go into the details of Edie's friendship with Rachel McCarthy, the murdered girl.

"He should be working the night shift. I'll give him a call and let him know you'll be there in about half an hour, if that's all right.''

"That's fine,'' I replied. "Thanks, Lee.''

"Mac can bypass the red tape for you and hook you up with someone in Missing Persons.''

That was great. It meant that Edie's case would be taken more seriously. Not that the police ever did anything but take missing persons cases seriously, especially missing children, but we wouldn't have to go through numerous channels and countless interviews before they got around to investigating. I thanked Lee and hung up.

Before I could grab my stuff and get out the door, the phone rang once more. Reaching over, I hit the on switch for my answering machine to screen the call.

After the beep, I heard, "Angela, this is your mother. Are you there?''

Oh, God. Ma. What was I going to tell Ma about Rosa? Did she even have to know? In either case, I couldn't talk to her right now. I resolved to call her back later. After Rosa and I had gotten our stories straight.

IT WAS AFTER seven when I got to the Revere police station. A tightly strung Ev was waiting for me in the enclosed lobby. Plain wooden benches hugged the walls, with iron loops set waist-high for handcuffing uncooperative suspects. Ev was wearing his B uniform with all the medals and doodads that he had accrued over his years in the service. It looked impressive and I understood immediately that that was the point. He wanted to be taken seriously, and the uniform would almost guarantee that. He stood up when I came in, and from his demeanor I could tell that being here was difficult for him. I felt doubly bad about being late. He must have seen it in my face, because he made an effort to relax.

"Sorry, Ev," I said. "I got a call in my office just as I was getting ready to leave."

I didn't bother to explain more than that. Instead, I walked up to the desk sergeant and asked if Detective MacMillan was in. A moment later, the sergeant buzzed us through the door and we were met by a tall, whip-thin man in his forties. He wore his long shirtsleeves rolled up to the elbows, and his tie had been loosened as if it had been a long day for him. His reddish walrus mustache made up for the receding hairline and pitted face. Still, he was attractive in an Edward James Olmos sort of way.

"I'm Detective MacMillan," he said, holding out his hand to me. I shook it, noting that his hands were callused, as if he worked outdoors instead of at a desk. While I made the introductions, Ted MacMillan eyed me curiously. "Randolph told me about you. Ex-marine?"

I hadn't been paying much attention to anything but Ev's missing daughter, but now I looked close and recognized a fellow marine. Ev had probably already pegged him. It was sort of like recognizing someone who belonged to the same secret brotherhood you belonged to. MacMillan nodded to us to follow him.

"Lee filled me in on your case," he said, glancing at Ev sympathetically. "How old is she?"

A muscle in Ev's jaw twitched. "Fourteen just last month."

"She was best friends with the girl who was found on Revere Beach," I added.

MacMillan stopped short. "The McCarthy girl? That happened a few days ago. And she was missing for almost a week when we found her. How come a missing report hasn't been filed for this other girl yet?"

Ev and I filled him in as much as we could while MacMillan led us through a maze of cubicles. He was frowning by the time we reached the far corner of the room. A compact clean-shaven black man looked up from his computer. Wearing a neatly pressed light-blue shirt and dark-print tie, he looked like he was just a couple of years out of the academy. He must have moved up the ladder quickly, because they usually kept rookies on patrol for five years.

MacMillan introduced us. "I'm going to leave you in Detective Holmes's capable hands." The nameplate on the detective's desk told me that his first name was Robert.

Holmes smiled pleasantly and gestured to two empty chairs. When Ev and I were situated, I opened up with, "You must get a lot of kidding about your last name."

Holmes rolled his eyes and grinned. "Yeah, everything from 'Your first name's not Sherlock, is it?' to 'Where's Watson?' It gets old, but it could be worse."

"You could have been named Buttafuoco and be working Vice," I replied. Holmes chuckled, and I could feel Ev's tension lessen a bit. We got the preliminaries out of the way, and I turned over the diary to the detective. He wasn't thrilled that I'd gone into Edie's room, but he was happy to have the evidence. Ev gave me a wounded look. I returned it with a we'll-discuss-this-later look. He didn't seem very satisfied.

Before long, Ev was telling his story to Detective Holmes. I picked it up with a report of my investigation and where it had led. Holmes was frowning when I finished. He turned the tape recorder off. "I'll get this transcribed and have you go over the report tomorrow to make sure nothing was left out." He turned to me. "Since you were hired to find Edie, is it your intention to continue?"

I wasn't sure how to answer that. It wasn't standard procedure for a private investigator to work a case that was considered open by the police. Ev answered before I could formulate a response. "I would consider it a favor if you let Ms. Matelli continue, Detective."

"As long as I don't interfere with your investigation," I quickly added, "and keep you informed of any information I get that would be deemed helpful.''

Holmes had been toying with a pen, twirling it back and forth in his fingers. ''It's definitely not by the book, but then''—he looked up at me as if considering my status carefully—''this is an unusual case. You were brought in first, but I'd appreciate it if you'd give us a day or two to make a preliminary investigation.''

''That sounds fair,'' I said.

Ev reluctantly nodded in agreement. ''The sooner she's back on the case, the better.''

''I agree. The trail grows colder by the day,'' Holmes continued, ''so let's not allow for more than a few days before you get back on the case.''

I thought of something else, a way for me to stay on the case. ''What about Rachel McCarthy? Have you come up with any suspects?''

Holmes frowned and shook his head. ''I worked on it when she was a missing case, but when her body was found, all our work was turned over to Homicide. You should ask Mac. He's on that detail.''

We shook hands on it. I liked this man. He was still in his midtwenties, but he had enough confidence to not let his ego get in the way of a young girl's life.

A slow smile spread across his features. He shook my hand, then Ev's.

''I'll have to go over and interview your ex-wife,'' he added apologetically. ''I'd appreciate it if you would put off any visit with her until I've seen her.'' It went without saying that Holmes considered her a suspect in Edie's disappearance, as were all people connected with Edie. Even Ev wasn't immune from investigation, and I was certain he knew that.

While Ev stayed back at Holmes's desk and answered some probing questions, I wandered over to MacMillan's desk on the other side of the room. I felt lucky to find him in. If we'd been in Charlestown, chances of finding him still here would have been slim, but Revere wasn't quite as tough a neighborhood. There was crime, but Charlestown's sort of faceless, terror-inducing violence hadn't penetrated Revere yet.

MacMillan was sitting on the edge of his desk, eating what looked like turkey and lettuce with mustard on whole wheat. A carton of yogurt sat next to a can of Coke on his desk.

"Detective MacMillan?"

He looked up at me, his eyes bleary from reading badly typed reports. I noticed the file name on the manila folder: McCarthy, R. He noticed my interest.

"Just catching up on some unsolved cases," he said, sliding off the desk and going around to sit properly, pulling his half-eaten sandwich across the desk in front of him.

"Please go on eating." I sat on the other side of the desk.

"These cases with kids"—he gestured to Rachel McCarthy's file—"really get to me." I noticed the black-and-white glossies of Rachel's body. He'd been studying the crime scene, hoping to pick out a detail, something he hadn't noticed the first hundred times he'd looked at it.

"What can I do for you?"

"It's what I can do for you," I replied. "I know Detective Holmes will be telling you all this and more, but I thought I'd give you the information first-hand." I told him about the suspected connection between Rachel and Edie.

MacMillan listened silently, taking down notes as the story unfolded. When I was finished, he sat back and studied me. "Thanks for the info. I don't know how much good it's going to do."

"What did you have before this?"

"Nothing," he admitted. "No one came forward to admit that they had seen Rachel before she disappeared. No one, that is, except her teachers. She left school that day, September thirtieth, and just disappeared into thin air." I was surprised that he was talking to me about the case, especially here in the squad room. But I could hear the frustration in his voice.

"This never gets easy, does it?"

MacMillan looked away for a moment, his expression neutral. Just the twitch of a jawline muscle and the flare of his nostrils gave away his impatience at not solving this one. "She was molested. The look on her face was—" He fell silent and looked down at his sandwich, finally pushing it away. There was no need to elaborate; I had seen the expression on her face, what was left of it. The rest of the body was remarkably well-preserved for having washed up on the beach.

"How long was her body in the ocean?" I asked.

MacMillan consulted his file notes. "Not long. There was dirt in her hair as if she'd been buried somewhere, then dug up." He chewed on a fingernail for a moment, staring over my left shoulder.

"So she wasn't drowned? The reporting was vague." I knew why. Some details need to be kept from the public so that the killer might give himself away.

"There was no sea water in her lungs," Mac said. "The ME thinks she might have been suffocated." Suddenly, he asked, "You're not thinking of pursuing this, are you?"

I frowned. As I said, it wasn't good etiquette to get in the way of a police investigation. Still, it did seem as if our paths would cross. And honesty is still the only policy I subscribe to when it comes to police relations. "It's so relevant to Edie Morrow's disappearance that I don't see how I can stay out of it." Before he could counter, I added, "Everett Morrow is a friend of mine. I can't give up the case now. Not the case of a fellow marine."

MacMillan didn't say anything for a minute. Then he sat up and nodded brusquely, his eyes wary. "All right. Lee Randolph says you're okay. As long as you stay out of our way and give us anything relevant to the case, by all means stay on it."

I maintained a level expression, not giving way to the jaw-dropping exhilaration I felt. MacMillan had pretty much given me the go-ahead. I knew it was partly because I was a fellow marine and partly because it was a missing, possibly dead, kid. Not even the police want to fight over territorial rights to cases where the best interests of the child should come first.

I made a silent note to ask MacMillan if, after this case was finished, he wanted to join our Friday night poker game.

TEN

IT WAS ALMOST 8:30 p.m. when we left the station. Ev had taken a cab to Revere, so I drove him back to his hotel in Somerville.

Actually, I'd use any excuse to drive my new car, a gray '95 Chevy Corsica. Ever since my Datsun 510's engine died, I'd been bemoaning my auto-less fate. Then I saw an ad in the *Boston Phoenix* for this car. The owner just needed someone to take over the payments.

There was a real difference in the way a '90s car handled as opposed to my old '70s car. Corsicas weren't top of the line, but that was all right with me. I was looking for a car that didn't stand out in a crowd, and the Corsica fit right in. It also had some handy features, such as the little reading lights on the rearview mirror and the fact that the backseat folds down for access to the trunk from inside.

We were heading for the southbound entrance of the East Boston Expressway when Ev finally spoke. "Why didn't you show me the diary before turning it over to the police?"

"What, you never heard of a photocopy machine?" I asked as I pulled out a sheaf of papers and gave it to him.

He tried to read them, but it was too dark and he soon gave up. I didn't bother to tell him about the reading light on the rearview mirror. "What does she talk about?"

"You, her mother," I said. "She kind of figured out that Earlene lied to her. But Edie is concerned about her mother. She thinks she needs to take care of her because there's no one else."

"Earlene can—" he stopped and caught his breath. I looked over and saw a pale version of a smile on Ev's face. "I really appreciate what you're doing for me, Ange."

"Hey, no problem."

We'd been silent for a few minutes when Ev dropped a bombshell. "I want to see Earlene."

"You heard what Detective Holmes said," I replied evenly. "Besides, I don't think that would be such a good idea, Ev. Not now. Wait until we find Edie." *Then you can beat up her mother,* I thought. In the dim glow of the passing streetlights, I could see the anger and impotence on his face.

But Marine training teaches us to detach and think logically in an impossible situation. I could almost hear the wheels turning in Ev's mind. I decided to nudge him a little in the right direction. "You're a suspect, too, Ev. If you confront Earlene before the police interview her, they won't be very happy." And I wanted to keep the police happy right now.

"I don't give a damn if it makes them unhappy," he replied, although there wasn't much heart in his voice.

"At least give them until tomorrow to talk to her. And like I said, when you do go to see her," I reminded him softly, "I want to be there. I know you'll control yourself, but I'd feel better if I were there with you.''

Ev grunted, obviously not in the mood to talk to me since I was being obstinate about Earlene. I decided a change in subject might take his mind off of Edie, so I told him about Rosa.

When I was finished, he was almost chuckling. "She must be a lot like you."

I shrugged. "Of course she is. She's my sister." I pulled up to the hotel entrance, and Ev turned to me.

"I don't mean just in the looks department. I mean she must be, you know—"

"Crazy?" I ventured. "Tough? Headstrong?"

Ev thought a moment. "Something like that."

I shook my head. "She's none of those things. She wouldn't last a day on Parris Island. I don't know; she's a little naive, but I guess we're similar in some ways. But my other sister, Sophia—now, she's another story.''

"I remember stories about her when we were working together. Has she changed at all?"

I thought about that question for a moment. Normally, I wouldn't hesitate to say no, she hadn't changed. But she was different these days. "She seems to have found her Prince Charming," I replied slowly. "The only problem is, he's married."

"And what about you, Angie?" Ev asked. "Have you found your Prince Charming?"

Our eyes met. He had a nice smile when he smiled. I hoped he had a lot to smile about in the near future. I wanted things to work out for him and for Edie.

I grinned. "I haven't been looking for him real hard.''

"Can you stay and have a drink with me?"

I had so much to do that I felt as if the night wasn't long enough. I wanted to stay, but getting involved with clients while trying to find their missing daughters was probably frowned upon in the rule book for private investigators. Still, I could see the loneliness and pain in Ev's eyes. It was hard to say no.

"Gee, Ev," I said slowly, "I'd like to, but can we do it another night? Rosa's at home, waiting to give me her reports."

Ev looked at me with amusement. "I'll have to meet your family someday, Angie. They sound like nice people."

I smiled. "Screwy, but nice." We parted on a pleasant note, and I drove back to Eastie, the common nickname for East Boston.

I wasn't sure if Rosa was still at the precinct or if she had gone home. I stopped at a gas station to fill my tank and called Rosa's home number. She answered.

"When did you get in?" I asked.

"About an hour ago. Detective Randolph was real nice. When're you coming home, Sarge?"

"I'm on my way."

Half an hour later, I was sitting on Rosa's couch in her apartment, listening to her account of what happened.

"I followed Betty DaSilva, just like I was supposed to," Rosa began. "She was using a cane, walking with a kind of shuffle. We went to the grocery store where she bought three bags of groceries, and a bag boy carried them out to her car. Then we went to the mall, where she got one of those little

motorized golf carts to wheel around in. I had a hard
time keeping up with her.'' Rosa let out a sigh and
shifted her position on the couch, tucking her feet up
underneath her legs.

"I still don't see how you ended up being arrested," I said.

Rosa went on as if she hadn't heard me. "She
bought some stuff at a kitchen and linen store and at
a bookstore, and picked up her medication at a drugstore. Then she bought a pair of running shoes and
a jogging outfit at an athletic store. Then she got back
in her car and I followed her to a nice jewelry store
in Brookline. That's where I was picked up."

"Where were you?"

"Outside the store."

"Right outside?"

"Yeah, I was trying to look like I was just win-
dow-shopping."

"Jewelry stores don't like window-shoppers,
Rosa. How long was she in there?"

"About an hour."

"An hour? You window-shopped one store window for an hour?" I tried not to let my amazement
show, but it was inevitable. Rosa's bottom lip began
to tremble. God, I didn't need to make her cry.
"Now, hold on, sis. Don't go soft on me."

"I tried, Sarge, I really did. How could I be so
stupid?" Rosa punched a pillow halfheartedly.

I closed my eyes to calm myself, wishing I'd been
able to go to the dojo tonight. But I felt weird about
Dave. I wasn't sure I could face him again this week.
At least, not until Sunday. I still wasn't sure what I
was going to do about that.

Why was I the one who always ended up putting out the fires? Then I thought back to the cause of the current troubles among the Matelli sisters—Sophia would never have become involved with Dave if I hadn't introduced them; Rosa wouldn't be in this hot water if I hadn't taken her on as an intern. It *was* all my fault! That's why I was the one with the fire hose.

"I guess I just lost track of the time," Rosa muttered. "Or maybe she spotted me." She brightened a bit. "I think that's it, Sarge. I think Betty DaSilva spotted me!" She was so happy, I didn't point out that it wasn't a good thing.

"It's called 'being made,'" I replied.

"That's what happened. I noticed her looking back at me several times, but I always tried to act casual." I could just picture it—this DaSilva woman glances behind her and sees Rosa studying a blank wall, or trying to read the back of a condom packet at the drugstore. I choked back a giggle. Rosa was still talking. "I kept filming her, though."

I perked up. "Then let's look at the tape."

Rosa got up and staggered to the closet. "Ooh, my feet fell asleep. Yeah, here it is." She produced the briefcase. As she struggled with the locks, she said, "The police tried to open it, but I told them I didn't have the combination, that it was my husband's briefcase and he'd forgotten it this morning at home." At least she was good at making up a story on the spur of the moment.

The briefcase came open with a little force and Rosa extracted the tape from the camera. We popped it in her VCR and played it, Rosa giving me the remote to fast-forward through dull stuff. I noted that the DaSilva woman had the shifty look of someone who knows she's being followed. I wasn't sure if she'd made Rosa until the jewelry store incident, but it was clear that she had something on her mind. I was intrigued by the fact that she bought clothes and shoes for jogging, trying them on to make sure they fit. Maybe she had a sister or friend the same size and was giving the items to her as a gift, or maybe she intended to get more exercise when she felt better. Either way, I had a day to take over and find out.

I watched the shaky, amateur picture, fast-forwarding through most of it. Mrs. DaSilva moved slowly, and always made sure a salesperson bent to pick up things she couldn't reach. The woman Rosa had followed had either been telling the truth or was very good at acting like a woman with a bad back.

However, I had done a little background investigation on Mrs. DaSilva before handing over this assignment to Rosa, and I was betting on the latter. The woman had a history of pulling this sort of stunt. I'd have to find some time to follow up on this case myself, now that Rosa wasn't sure what she wanted to do. I was pretty sure that her time in jail had discouraged her from continuing in this line of work. I only hoped that it didn't get back to Ma anytime soon. She'd ream me out for not protecting her youngest.

I got up, grabbed the briefcase and video camera, and extracted the tape from the VCR. "Thanks, Rosa. I'll take over tomorrow."

"But Sarge—"

"You have to write up a report tomorrow morning—and besides, she made you already." I gave her a hug. "You did a good job, kiddo. There's a few things about shadowing someone that you need to know, but other than a few technical things, you did good. We'll go over it tomorrow morning, okay?"

When I got back to my apartment, it was quiet—no crisis to avert, no stress to handle, and nothing to eat in my refrigerator. I was starving, but for once, I didn't feel like going out to fuel my body. I found a jar of hazelnut spread and a box of soda crackers.

While I was enjoying this gourmet treat, washing it down with a beer, I began to wish that I had a pet to come home to. Maybe I'd look into it later. I liked cats and dogs, but I couldn't see owning one. Too much trouble. I wanted a pet that wouldn't require feeding more than once a week and didn't shed its skin.

It was a little after ten o'clock, but I wanted to call Rachel McCarthy's parents and set up an appointment to talk to them. Detective MacMillan had agreed that since the investigation into the little girl's murder was going nowhere, I could contact the McCarthys in an unofficial capacity. I tried the number he had given me for them. When their answering machine picked up I left my name and number for them to call me back.

I called my office to access my new answering machine—I had two messages. Sometimes I like to play a little game with myself: How many of these messages are from my family? I decided both of them—one from Ma and one from Sophia. But surprisingly, the first one was from Earlene.

"Uh, this is for Angela Matelli." I could tell that she wasn't comfortable talking into answering machines. "Anyway, tell her that I'll be going to the police station to file a missing persons report tomorrow."

I decided to call her back and hung up before accessing the second message. Detective Holmes might call on her tonight, but he might wait until tomorrow. Either way, she needed to be aware that the report had been filed and she would be interviewed.

I dialed her number and let it ring. Eight rings later, she picked up. I recognized her voice from the slur in it. She was feeling good. "H'lo?"

"Earlene? This is Angela Matelli. I got your message and wanted to return your call." I paused to get a response, but all I got was a muffled heavy breathing on the other end of the phone. "Anyway, I thought you should know that Ev went down to the station and filed a missing child report. It's already been done, so you don't have to do it. But I think the detective on the case, Robert Holmes, will be in contact with you tonight or tomorrow."

I waited again, hearing only the breathing on the other end. "Earlene?" I ventured, "are you there?"

Her voice came out low and gravelly. "Yeah, I'm here." I thought I detected a bit of sarcasm, and I soon found out I was right. "Not that anyone would notice. Who the hell are you and Ev to take over like that? Edie's my responsibility here in Massachusetts, not his. And it's none of your goddamn business."

I didn't have to answer because she slammed the phone down in my ear. Geez, try to do someone a favor and what do you get for your trouble? I was beginning to wonder if she'd gotten word about Ev's coming to town. Maybe she had Edie hidden somewhere. Earlene didn't act like a mom whose child was missing.

I thought back to earlier days, when she had still been lucid. Earlene had always been paranoid about losing Ev—and from the way things had gone in the last few years, she certainly had good reason—but she had never been as out of control as she seemed to be now. Her drug use had been limited to prescription pills, although she did chug down the liquor on a regular basis. I sighed, shook my head, and decided to deal with Earlene tomorrow. It was late and I was tired. But I still had another call to play back. I had figured that both messages were from my family, and at least on this second one I was right. I called my machine again and heard:

"Angie, this is your mother. I just wanted to call and talk to you, but you're never home. What is it with you? I'm cursed with children who neglect me!"

I hung up, let out a big sigh, and deliberated for a moment, then came to the conclusion that since I was such a bad daughter, I'd neglect Ma for just a few more hours in favor of some sleep.

ELEVEN

THE PROBLEM WAS THAT I couldn't get any sleep. I
kept tossing and turning. It probably didn't help that
it had started to rain, and the pounding of drops on
my tar-and-metal rooftop sounded like fingers cease-
lessly drumming.

Every time I squeezed my eyes together, Edie
haunted me. I saw her face from the photo Ev had
given me and remembered the lively seven-year-old
girl I'd played hide-and-seek with in the Morrows'
backyard.

And if I didn't see Edie, I saw Rachel McCarthy's
body washed up on Revere Beach. It was almost two
in the morning when I finally got up and decided
now would be a good time to go see Bobbie Matthews, Earlene's oversexed roommate. Earlene had
told me that she worked the graveyard shift as a waitress at a truckstop on Route 1, and I figured this was
as good a time as any to go see her. It probably
wouldn't be too busy, not at this hour of the morning.

The restaurant where Bobbie Matthews worked
was easy to get to—I just stayed on Route 1 until I
got to Revere and got off when I saw the pink-and-
blue neon sign. It actually said LOU S P ACE, but I got
the idea. Inside, the decor ran to bad '70s motifs:
dark Mediterranean wood trim, coffee-stained or-
ange-plastic upholstered booths and chairs, fake plastic Tiffany hanging lamps that emitted a sickly yel-

low twenty-watt glow, Hank Williams on the jukebox.

I almost didn't recognize Bobbie with her clothes on, but she was the only waitress in the place. I'd seen way too many people with their clothes off lately. I must have done something wicked in a former life.

Naturally, *she* didn't recognize *me* when she came up to take my order. I scanned the joint and was surprised at the number of people who were up at this hour. Most of them seemed to be truck drivers, but a few rheumy-eyed drunks were slumped over a cup of coffee, trying to sober up before going home to the missus.

Bobbie was a chubby redhead—whether it was natural or not was only something she and Clairol would know. I hadn't looked that close. She wore her hair in a retro bouffant do and had taken care to put on lots and lots of makeup—black mascara applied so thick that if she batted her eyelashes, it would stun any flying insect that came within reach; foundation that didn't disappear into her skin, but was applied with all the subtlety of road tar; and frosty petal-pink lipstick that shimmered and glistened like shiny spandex when she smiled. She cracked gum with the best of them and had a not-so-natural beauty mark à la Cindy Crawford. Her fragrance was Hit You over the Head Honeysuckle.

I sized her up as the type of woman who really likes men and enjoys sex and doesn't take either too seriously. Assessing Bobbie wasn't too much of a stretch for me, having seen her doing the wild thing on the couch in front of her kids. ''What can I gitcha,

honey?'' She cocked one fleshy hip out—I would
have thrown mine out if I'd tried that—and began to
write in her ticket book. First, I ordered a tuna sandwich and a root beer float. Then I introduced myself.

She arched painted-on brows. ''Oh, you're the one
Em was talking about. I suppose you want to ask
some questions. Anything that might help Em.'' I
wasn't sure what that meant, but I noticed that while
Em was important to Bobbie, Edie's name was never
mentioned. Well, I'd already seen that she wasn't too
concerned about her own kids.

Bobbie scanned the restaurant to make sure her
customers were taken care of. Most of them had
drifted away, leaving money with their checks by
their empty plates and mugs. Several customers were
still seated but were snoozing over their coffee. One
fellow was even snoring.

''Do you need to go wake him?'' I asked.

''Nah,'' she said with a sneer. ''His wife told me
to just leave him here until he wakes up.'' She
snorted. ''More like when he sobers up. Let me go
put your order in; then I'll take a break and we can
talk.''

When she came back, she had made my root beer
float and set it in front of me. Unlike most places
that make floats with soft-serve ice cream these days,
this was the real thing—creamy and smooth with a
frozen crust of root beer covering the vanilla ice
cream. I tried not to salivate over it as I pulled the
straw out and licked off the ice cream.

I decided to stick to neutral territory until I got
more of a read on Bobbie. ''How did you meet Emily
and Edie?'' I referred to Earlene by the name she

had given Bobbie so there wouldn't be any confusion.

"Em and I met about two and a half months back. She and Edie came in here to use the phone. From the want ads she had spread out on the table, I could tell she was looking for a place to stay." Bobbie paused and shook her head. "Edie looked so tired and sad. I think she's the saddest child I've ever met."

I wouldn't exactly say that. I'd met Bobbie's kids, and she didn't have my vote for Mother of the Year either. But I kept silent, letting Bobbie talk. "Anyway, we got to talking, and Em and I had some things in common—"

I pressed my lips together to keep from blurting out that they were both lousy mothers and had creepy boyfriends.

"—and I couldn't keep up the rent on that house all by myself, ever since my former roomie did one of those midnight moves, sticking me with a three-hundred-dollar phone bill."

Again, I could barely keep my thoughts to myself, but at least I now suspected why Bobbie was so eager to help. She probably was afraid Earlene would get thrown in jail and wouldn't pay her rent if Edie wasn't found.

I ran through the list of suspects in my head. "Em gave me several names of people who had contact with Edie." I told her about the possible connection with Rachel McCarthy, and for the first time, I thought I saw a spark of sympathy in Bobbie's eyes.

"Oh, that poor little girl. I remember seeing her around the place a few times." Bobbie paused, her pencil tapping out a thoughtful staccato on her check pad, then added, "Edie was always really excited about seeing Rachel. The poor kid didn't seem to have a lot of friends. Kept to herself mostly. Didn't seem to care much for my kids." She shook her head, as if Edie had really missed out by being so antisocial.

"You can understand why I'm anxious to find Edie, then."

She opened her eyes wide. "Oh, yes. Of course. Whatever you want to know."

The cook rang the bell and she excused herself. After loudly proclaiming to one and all that she was going on break, she brought me a tired-looking tuna on toast with a side of potato chips—the cheap brand—and a couple of thin pickle slices. She also brought a mug of coffee for herself.

"What can you tell me about Em's relationship with her daughter?"

Bobbie leaned forward, waxing enthusiastic. "They were really close, those two. Em took good care of Edie, and Edie worshipped the ground her mother walked on."

I looked up at Bobbie, keeping my expression flat. She blinked a couple of times, then took a nervous sip of her coffee. I smiled and she smiled back. "Cut the crap, Bobbie. I knew Em seven years back, and she was an alcoholic then. Now she's an alcoholic and pill user. I saw a pill bottle. Come on. Be honest. It won't cost you anything."

Bobbie pulled a flattened pack of Virginia Slims out of her apron pocket and lit one. I was sitting in the no-smoking area, but this was no time to complain. After exhaling a long stream of smoke, she looked down at her mug.

"Okay, you're right. Em and Edie were at it constantly. Edie hated her life, hated me, hated my kids. She was constantly on her mother about improving their lives, getting off the booze and pills. But she didn't understand."

I bit. "What didn't she understand?"

Bobbie looked at me in earnest. "We can't do any better than low-paying jobs and kids to raise. It isn't possible."

Of course, getting off booze and drugs would be a start, but it wasn't worth the effort to point that out. Besides, I wasn't a therapist or counselor. I was a PI looking for a missing kid.

"Why didn't Edie just call her dad up and have him come get her? Or why didn't she run away?"

Bobbie blew a dangling lock of hair from in front of her eyes. "I wasn't supposed to hear this, but one day I came home from my shift early, and I heard Em tell Edie that her dad had gone on a secret military mission that had taken him out of the country. That they had agreed that Edie would live with her mother. A week later, I hear Edie talking to Rachel on the phone, telling her that she thought her mom was lying to her."

"Wow," was all I could say. It was a pretty elaborate lie for Earlene, but at least she hadn't used the old standard line about how her dad hadn't wanted her anymore.

I brought the conversation back to Rachel. "Did you ever talk to Rachel?"

"Heavens, no," Bobbie replied, fluttering her eyelashes. "There was no reason to."

I didn't know where I was going with this, but it helped to get a full picture of Edie's life and her relationships.

"I don't think her parents approved of her being at our house." Bobbie rolled her eyes like there was something wrong with the McCarthys for thinking that way. "She seemed like a nice girl, very close to Edie. They usually spent their time holed up in Edie's room. Once or twice Stick gave them money to go to a movie."

"You did notice that Edie wasn't around this past week, didn't you?"

Bobbie flinched. I wasn't sure if her reaction was from the tendrils of smoke curling up from the cigarette that lay on the saucer in front of her, or from my question.

Her eyes slid away from me, which answered my unspoken question. "I didn't notice until recently."

"When exactly?"

She picked up her cigarette and waved it around for effect. "Oh, you know. There's so many kids around our place, it's hard for me to pinpoint." Bobbie looked around the restaurant again as if she wanted an escape route. Guilt was uncomfortable to wear.

I changed the subject slightly, wanting to keep her off balance. I'd get an answer to that question later. "What about the others who were around during that time?" I thought back to my short list of suspects. "What about Em's friend, Stick? You know his real name?"

She shrugged. "We just always called him Stick. I think I heard someone once use his last name—Fallon."

"What's your impression of him?"

Bobbie looked serious. "Don't mess with him," she said in a low voice.

I was going to answer her, but then realized that this was her impression of him. "Okay, why do you say that?"

For the first time, I saw fear in her eyes. "I heard that he broke a man's hand once for arguing with him about where his bike was parked. I guess the guy didn't like the fact that Stick parked his hog across the guy's private driveway."

I made a mental note of that: Go ahead and let Stick park his Harley wherever the hell he pleased. "What was his relationship with Edie?"

"He seemed to like her all right. He sometimes brought her little gifts like a bracelet or a Gameboy." A Gameboy didn't seem like such a little gift to me, and my brain began to percolate: Where was Stick getting this stuff? How much of it was hot? Bobbie continued, "I could tell she didn't really take to him, though. But she was polite enough around him."

"And Joe Blount?"

Her face expressed distaste. "My ex-boyfriend."

"How long did you see him?"

"We were going out when Em and Edie came to live with me." I noticed she said me, not us. Apparently, Bobbie's kids were nonessential. "Edie knew him fairly well. He spent a good deal of time in the house. Sometimes he'd be there on his mornings off, waiting for me to come in from my shift. She'd be getting ready for school.''

"What does he do for a living?''

"Welder. Works off and on in the contracting business. Business hasn't been so good lately.'' She smirked and added, "That's what he says, but I've heard other people tell me he isn't reliable and he's too weird to work with.''

"What do you think?'' I asked. "You went out with him.''

She shrugged. "He was okay. I just think he lived with his mother too long. She died last year, and he still lives in the same crummy little house. I would have sold it in a heartbeat and gotten a nice condo.''

Yeah, the day I'd take financial advice from Bobbie Matthews was the day I'd get me a waitress job at a truckstop diner. "Herb Cooper. What's he like?''

Bobbie's face lit up. "He's, well, he's my current guy.'' I figured he was the guy on the sofa with Bobbie the other day. I suppressed a shudder. It was truly an event I hoped not to witness again. Bobbie frowned, as if she'd remembered something not so pleasant. "Of course, he's married, so you can't interview him.''

We'd see about that. "So tell me what he's like. Where did you meet him?''

A reluctant grin spread across her face. "I went country line dancing a couple of months ago with Joe. We were almost ready to split—at least, I was—and I met Herb during a partner exchange. We really hit it off.''

"Did he ever meet Edie?''

Bobbie blinked her spider-leg eyelashes. "Sure. A

few times.'' Her noncommittal expression told me there was more to the story, but I probably would have to get it elsewhere.

I raised my eyebrows, maintaining silence. Bobbie seemed nervous as she ground out her cigarette.

She lit another and blew her smoke upward, watching its blue stream reach for the ceiling. ''Any more questions?''

''When was the last time you saw Edie?''

''I think it was last Friday morning when she left for school. About seven-thirty.''

''And when was the last time you saw Rachel?''

She was beginning to shift in her seat, looking impatient to get back to work. ''I don't remember.''

''What does Herb do for a living?''

''He owns a print shop.'' Her eyes narrowed into two thick black lines. ''You're not thinking of involving him in this, are you?''

I told her I wouldn't dream of it. Of course, I had my fingers crossed behind my back the whole time.

TWELVE

THE PHONE RANG at seven-thirty on Friday morning. I can be a bear to deal with in the morning, but fortunately I was already awake. It was Larry McCarthy.

"I'm afraid I don't remember who you are," he apologized.

I introduced myself and explained why I was calling. There was an audible sigh on the other end of the phone. "I hope you're not really another reporter trying to get an angle on the story," he said, quickly adding, "Not that we couldn't use the publicity to goose the police into working on some different angles, but I don't know if my wife can go through this again."

"You can call Detective MacMillan at the precinct to verify my story," I offered. "Did you know Edie Morris?" I almost used her real last name, but caught myself in time. McCarthy wouldn't know her last name was really Morrow.

"Yes, we did. I always thought there was something a little sad about her," he said. "She never failed to bring up her dad when she came over to our house." I made a note of that. Ev would be happy to hear that she hadn't forgotten him or given up hope of ever seeing him again.

Larry McCarthy promised to get back to me as soon as he talked to MacMillan.

I was ready to pop Rosa's tape in the machine to
watch the fun again, but I remembered that Rosa had
told me that the DaSilva woman had bought a jogging outfit yesterday. And she had tried it on, which
meant it might well be for her. Hmmm. It would be
hard to resist trying out a designer jogging suit for
the first time. It was twenty to eight. Betty DaSilva
was on disability at the moment, but there was a
possibility that she kept hours similar to when she
was working.

Before I hurried out of my apartment, taking time
to grab the video camera and check to make sure it
was loaded, I called Lee Randolph and left a message
on his voice mail, asking him to do background
checks on my suspects. I normally do them myself,
but time was of the essence here, and I was pretty
sure that Lee would understand. Since tonight was
our poker night, I promised to take him to an early
dinner, if he had the time.

Betty DaSilva and her family lived in Winthrop,
which was an upper-class East Boston neighborhood.
Winthrop was on the peninsula above Eastie. In fact,
on a clear night if you walked to the end of Logan
Airport where the planes took off from the seaboard,
you could see Winthrop's lights twinkling in the distance across the water to the west.

The DaSilvas lived off of one of the main thor-
oughfares, Pleasant Street. It was close to Winthrop
Community Hospital, and also close to Ingleside
Park.

It was a balmy day, sea breezes and airplane ex-
haust coming off the Boston Harbor and mingling
with the scent of money—specifically, the Mercedes

sports car sitting in the driveway of the modest three-story town house. I was fortunate that Betty DaSilva hadn't decided to start her jog at seven-thirty in the morning, or I would have been out of luck. No, she popped out the door about ten after eight, not more than a few minutes after I found a parking space down the block from her. And she was wearing her designer jogging suit, fuschia with silver stripes down the sides.

It was such a sunny day, and her new white running shoes were like beacons—I almost had to squint when I brought the lens up to my eye and followed her at an easy pace down the block. When she turned left on Wheelock, I started my car again and followed slowly. The right turn almost caught me by surprise, it was so soon, but I managed to make it without incident. I found another parking space near the park and got out, following her into Ingleside and down a jogger's path.

A few minutes of that and I was winded. I walked quickly back to my car. I'd been to Ingleside Park once before, and I was pretty sure that the jogging path was a loop. Ten minutes later, a happy, healthy, athletic-looking Betty DaSilva power-walked out of the park, sweat glistening on her forehead and at the hollow of her throat. I know because I made sure to zoom in on her face.

It was pretty easy to figure out why Betty DaSilva was out and about. When she spotted Rosa yesterday, she no doubt assumed she had taken care of the insurance company by making their investigator. What she hadn't thought through was there would be more than one investigator on her case.

Back home, I watched the tape and was satisfied that I had the evidence to nail Betty DaSilva. I rewound the tape and called Leone Insurance.

"I'll send my secretary over later this morning to pick up the tape," Bob Leone told me after I gave him the report.

"Send her to my apartment, and make sure she brings me a check for my services," I replied. "You owe me for this job and the work I did for you last week." I didn't like to let my clients take me for granted. Bob was one of the worst. I had gone to school with him, had even dated him for a time, and I sometimes think he thinks it's all right to wait a few weeks to pay me. Me? I like cash on delivery.

I called Rosa next. She had just woken up.

"You're up early, Sarge," she said. I didn't bother to tell her I'd been up half the night. I told her about Betty DaSilva.

"So it was okay that I screwed up," she said.

I put a good face on her screw-up. "Probably the best thing you could have done. You acted as a decoy." I asked her to let in the insurance secretary and give her the tape.

"No problem," she replied, sounding almost chipper.

Then I got a phone call from Ev. "I didn't get any sleep last night," he told me. "Geez, Ange, I've read these diary entries over and over again. Was I a bad father?"

"Why do you say that?"

He sounded frustrated and tired and angry and a little drunk. "I let her go with that bitch. I should have saved her."

There was no sob at the end, but I could hear the anguish in his voice.

"Ev, how long have you been looking for her?"

"Since I found out she was missing, but—"

"And when I found Earlene and discovered Edie was missing again, what did you do?"

"I went to the police, but—"

"But what?" I asked. My question was met with silence. "Do you think you're some kind of psychic? Because if you are, buddy, you'd better join that psychic nine hundred line because you could help a hell of a lot of people."

"But maybe she wouldn't have gone with her mother if I'd warned her, if I'd been there for her."

I closed my eyes. *If I'd done this, if I'd done that.* What did it amount to but a bunch of bullshit self-pity? I questioned my own reaction to his raw emotions. The Italian in me wanted to mother him, cook him a good meal, nurture him. The marine in me, the side Ev knew best, was the reaction that surfaced when confronted with pain and guilt.

Either way, I was trying to be patient with Ev. He was hurting. He was blaming himself for something he couldn't have foreseen and couldn't control. I decided to play it straight with him.

"Look, we can do this two ways, Ev. I can play private eye and therapist to your self-loathing, but then I'd have to charge you twice and I'd do half as well at both jobs." Twice a dollar is two dollars, but who's counting? "Or I can just play private eye and help locate your daughter. I'll spend all my time at it, and I'm pretty damn good at this type of work."

"You're right as usual, Angie." His voice was frosty.

"Ev, wait. Look"—I softened my voice a bit—"I'm sorry I snapped at you. I have no idea what's happened to Edie. I can only hope this turns out all right. But you can't play these pity games with yourself. It'll eat you up and there won't be enough left over for your daughter when we find her."

I avoided using the "if" word: If we find her, if she's alive, if she's not emotionally scarred...

After we hung up, I didn't know what to do with myself, so I started cleaning the kitchen and bathroom floors, chores I hated to do. When you enter the military, you enter an institution that molds you, giving you detail-oriented habits you may not have had when you first signed on. I had never been a clean person when I was growing up, getting away with as few house chores as possible. I always had something more important to do. But the marines— or maybe it was old age creeping up on me—brainwashed me into accepting the fact that a floor sometimes needed to be swept and a dish needed to be washed. I also found cleaning to be a great way of clearing my mind of all the daily worries that interfere with my ability to free associate.

And of course, my mind did just that on this particular morning. I cleared away all thoughts of the impending Sunday dinner with Ma and concentrated on Rachel and Edie. I thought about Edie and Earlene and their tenuous relationship. I wondered again if Earlene was being straight with me or if she was playing some high-stakes game with Edie's life, sequestering her away from her father as punishment for the divorce. Earlene seemed to think she had reason to torment Ev.

It was about ten in the morning when the phone rang again. An apologetic Earlene was on the other end of the line.

"Sorry about yesterday's blowup," she said. I was surprised at how sober and subdued she sounded, but alcoholics are like Jekyll and Hyde—one moment, they sound as sane and responsible as any normal person, and the next, they're off on some wacky tantrum that only makes sense to them. Still, I decided to treat her as if this was normal, which for her, it was.

"Oh, that's all right," I replied. "You're going through a lot."

She sighed. "It's just that I feel so guilty that I didn't do anything when she disappeared. I—well, I guess I was feeling sorry for myself. I figured she'd left me for Ev, and I felt rejected. I know I'm not the best mother...." She trailed off as if she was waiting for me to protest to make her feel better. I just let it go.

"We're all under a lot of pressure," I said. "But we all want what's best for Edie, don't we? I know Ev probably jumped the gun by taking things into his own hands without consulting you, but you have to admit that his marine uniform probably got more attention to Edie's case than if you or I had gone in there alone."

Admitting to something I didn't really believe— that Ev had jumped the gun—made Earlene think I was on her side. The fact of the matter was that I was on Edie's side and no one else's.

"Ye-es, I guess you're right." Earlene paused on the phone, her breath coming out in loud gasps as if she had started to cry. I waited, sensing there was something she wanted to tell me. "Look, Angela, I know you're working for Ev on Edie's case, but is there any way you could share any information you come across with me?"

Boy, I should have known. She wanted it for free. Well, it wasn't any skin off my nose, but I wasn't sure Ev would feel the same way—and he was, for all intents and purposes, my paying client. "I'd be happy to, Earlene, but since Ev's my client, we'll have to clear it with him first."

She groaned. "You know how he is with me, Angela. He probably wants my head on a platter for what's happened with Edie." Earlene paused for a moment, gasping as if she had just realized something. "My God, if she was with that little McCarthy girl, she could be dead, too!"

No shit, Sherlock. I'd been aware of that notion ever since I found out the two girls were best friends. Still, I'd been suppressing that thought, hoping for the best. I wanted to find Edie alive for Ev's sake, for my sake. For Earlene's sake? Well, I hoped Edie was alive, but I'm not sure if I cared enough about Earlene to hope it for her sake.

I realized Earlene was sobbing over the phone. I could barely understand her muffled self-pity. "I probably killed my little girl. It's all my fault. I don't blame Ev for hating my guts."

I decided this was as good a time as any to ask her about Stick. It would save me legwork and speed up the process of interviewing if I could get an address out of Earlene. "Look, Earlene, I really need to talk with everyone who had any contact with Edie. I've already spoken to Bobbie, and I'd like talk to your boyfriend, Stick. He might have seen or heard something; maybe something will come to mind that doesn't seem important to him now, but that might help find Edie."

There were a few moments of listening to her sniffle and blow her nose, but she finally answered me. "Okay, it's just that Stick isn't the most sociable guy. He likes his privacy."

I assured her that I'd respect that, but I really needed to ask him some questions. "He hangs out at Mike's Bar and Grill. It's a pool hall in Charlestown. He should be there now."

I talked with Earlene for a few more minutes, trying to calm her down. I ended up promising to talk to Ev myself about giving her the same updates. I didn't think it would be a good idea for them to have any contact. I was almost positive Ev would end up killing her. I was about ready to kill her myself by the end of our conversation. I'd never encountered a more self-centered person. Her sole concern seemed to be what Ev thought of her.

In fact, the more I thought about it, the less I knew about Edie. I hoped I'd be able to fill in some details when Larry McCarthy called me back about meeting with him and his wife. I wanted to know about both girls, their relationship to each other, and people they might know, people they might go to.

I got the call from Larry McCarthy a few minutes after Earlene's call. He agreed to meet with me on Sunday. I knew that Ma would find some way of getting back at me if I didn't come to dinner. She usually had dinner ready about noon, and liked her kids to spend a few hours with her, which pretty much took up most of the afternoon. But the evening was free, and between us, we agreed on seven o'clock at their house in Revere.

After we hung up, I got in my car and left for Charlestown, hoping to catch Stick at the pool hall. Charlestown isn't the sort of town you want to get caught in, even on a Friday morning. Although I suppose Friday would be the best day to be there. There are probably more unsolved murders per capita in working class Irish-Catholic Charlestown than in all of the Boston metropolitan area. Over the last few years, the "Irish Mafia" has chosen to settle disputes and paybacks by murdering people in broad daylight. And they always get away with it because eyewitnesses won't talk for fear of retaliation.

At a little after eleven, I was in front of Mike's. It looked closed from the outside, but when I tried the front door, it opened easily. As I stepped inside I heard someone call out, "We're closed." The sound of a pool cue hitting balls across a green felt surface echoed from the back of the semidarkened room. The sour smell of bourbon, beer, and old smoke lingered in the cool, cheerless room.

"I'm looking for Stick." My eyes adjusted and I could make out a couple of figures in back. There was no light except from a window that looked out into an alley and what little that spilled in from the front windows.

"He's not here," came a reluctant voice. A large, heavy biker carrying a pool cue walked into the light from one of the windows. He had scars on his face that looked like someone had tried plastic surgery the hard way on him. "Who're you?" It came out as more of a challenge than a question.

"Angela," I replied, trying to keep my voice from shaking. I had wandered into one of the few places where people weren't attending mass. I heard the *pok* of a ball hitting another ball, then a curse, and knew that Stick was in the next room. He just didn't want to see me. "I came to talk to Stick." I started to walk past Biker Boy. "He ain't here," Biker Boy repeated, moving to block my way.

"I'd like to see for myself." I moved again and his hand shot out, grabbing my arm roughly.

"Leave now," he said, unmoved. He started to pull me backward, toward the front door. His meaty left hand had ahold of my left elbow.

Instinctively, I stepped behind him, grabbed his hand, pulled him around, and turned his wrist out and down, performing *kodagaeshi*. He went down like a badly wounded bull elephant in a crystal shop, sailing backward and crashing into a chair. The wood frame splintered and shattered into toothpick-size pieces.

I was admiring my handiwork when I heard a "Hey!" from behind me and a whistling sound. I was able to partly deflect the cue stick that came at me, but it still caught me hard across my shoulder blades, knocking the wind out of me and driving me to my knees. I tried to catch my breath and couldn't find it. For a moment, I wheezed like an asthmatic fighting for air; then I began to see pinprick stars. When I was on the edge of blacking out, my lungs suddenly filled with air, and I gasped like a fish thrown back into the water.

"You all right?" I heard a male voice ask. Slowly, I stood up and turned around. Stick was leaning on the pool cue that had caught me across my back. He laid his pool cue across a nearby table, crossed his arms, and cocked his head as if he were studying an interesting life form—namely me.

My voice came out higher than it usually does. "I just wanted to talk to you."

Stick was watching me through narrowed eyes. "I seen you before. You were at the house yesterday. Em mentioned you to me when I went back to make up with her."

Since Earlene had talked to him already, I couldn't very well lie about what I did for a living. "That's right. I'm a private investigator."

"You're the one that found out Edie was missing." He nodded approvingly. "Not that it didn't cause me some trouble."

I could imagine, but I didn't say anything. I was just making a mental note to check out the people I planned to interview before going over to see them. I didn't want to get caught by another pool stick.

Stick went on. "The police been by already, askin' questions." He pushed off from the bar and grabbed a chair, turning it around to straddle it. Great, now I was going to be interrogated. "What was that stuff you used just now, some kind of karate?"

I decided it was better to answer his question without the smart talk. I had the feeling I was talking to someone who could seriously hurt me, aikido or no aikido.

"Aikido. It's purely self-defense." I risked a question. "I just need to talk to you about the last time you saw Edie. Can you tell me?"

He nodded. "It was about a week ago—a Friday, I think. She'd just returned from school and was doing her homework."

"Did you talk to her?"

He waited, but I was better at the waiting game. During our silence, I heard my biker friend stir and groan. I heard a chair scrape as he tried to stand up. Finally, Stick answered me. "Yeah, I usually don't, but she looked up as I passed her room. I asked how things were going, and she told me she was waiting for a friend. Then she told me she was going home and no one could stop her. I told her she was already home. She shook her head as if I was the dumbest guy in the world." He was almost smiling at the thought. I noticed that his lank hair was damp in the front and scraggly on the back of his neck.

"You want me to get the bitch, Stick?" I heard Biker Boy ask. I thought I detected a tremor in his voice, but that was probably just my imagination.

Stick shook his head in his lackey's direction, wordlessly gesturing for him to leave the room.

"Geez, lady," I heard Biker Boy address me, "all I was gonna do was escort you out the door. This is private property, you know."

I tossed a "Sorry" over my shoulder. With as much dignity as I could muster, I thanked Stick and told him I'd be in touch if I had any more questions. He seemed amused by the thought as I walked out the door.

As I crossed the street, I saw a white van pull into

the alley next to Mike's Pool Hall. The guys who got out didn't look like the sort I really wanted to meet, so I hurried to the Corsica and hoped they were too busy doing business with Stick to notice me.

I already had the call in to Lee Randolph, and I had a feeling Lee's computer would spit out some interesting stuff on this guy Stick. But I also worked partly on instinct, and my gut was telling me that even if this guy was into heavy shit, he wasn't involved in Edie's disappearance. He seemed to genuinely like Earlene, however stormy their relationship was, and when he talked about Edie, it was as if he thought of her as a little sister. Guys like Stick didn't do in family members—they did in guys who tried to whack their family members.

THIRTEEN

WHEN I HAD reassured myself that I hadn't been followed by thugs with machine guns, I started to breathe easier. My back still hurt from the pool cue, but I was pretty proud of myself for getting out of the situation without my gun. I conjured up an image of aikido class and felt guilty all over again for avoiding it. I'd have to see Dave on Sunday anyway, but I couldn't make myself go back to the dojo just yet.

I stopped at home and had lunch with Rosa. Leone's secretary had picked up the tape and left a substantial check for me. I stopped at a bank to deposit it, then took Rosa out to lunch to celebrate. We went to Casa Mia, a restaurant in Day Square.

"What do you want me to do now, Sarge?" she asked between spoonfuls of minestrone.

"Go back to my office and open up. Take messages," I instructed, not sure what else to have her do. I hadn't gotten any calls from Bob Leone or the repo company since yesterday. I made a mental note to call some of my regular customers and find out if there was a repo to pick up or a summons to serve.

Rosa noticeably drooped in her chair. "Couldn't I help you with your case?"

I remembered Rosa in jail. And I remembered Ma and the fact that she didn't know that Rosa had spent a couple hours in the slammer. I shook my head.

"There's not much you can do at the moment," I replied. "But I'll let you know if anything else needs to be done."

Rosa moped through the rest of the meal, but she perked up when I handed over her first paycheck and she studied it.

"Wow, I had no idea private investigation paid so well."

So, okay, I gave her a little extra because she was my sister and had landed in jail. Nepotism isn't dead. So sue me.

As I paid the check, I made a decision. "Okay, if any repo work comes in, you can do that."

"Repo work?"

I knew I was going to regret this, but Rosa was a big girl. "It can be dangerous if you don't do it right," I said, "but there's always two people doing it, so just follow the instructions you're given by whomever you work with. Just tell him you're new. Repo work involves surveillance if the client has hidden the car. And sometimes it means you go pick up a car at two in the morning."

"Okay, Sarge," Rosa said, giving me a two-finger salute. "I'll man the phones and repo the cars."

"Thanks, kid." I left the restaurant.

I decided it was a good time to go interview Herb Cooper, Bobbie's main squeeze. She'd told me where his print shop was located—on Broadway in Everett, which is way too close to Medford for my liking. I always feel guilty about being that close to Ma and not visiting her. But I kept telling myself that I was there on business, not to socialize.

Herb had quite the imagination—his business was

called Herb's Print Shop. It was small, but well
placed in Everett's business district in an outside
minimall. He probably had a loyal clientele. The
small parking lot out front of his shop had only a
black Chevy pickup parked in front, so I gathered he
wasn't busy at the moment.

A little bell rang when I walked into his shop. A
door led to a back room where I could hear heavy
machinery running. I was surprised to see a Webb
press beyond the opening—one of my uncles owns
a print shop that I'd worked at one summer during
high school. I had expected Herb to own a smaller
print shop—Webb presses did the bigger jobs like
books and large posters.

A six-foot guy in his late forties or early fifties
came to the front, wiping his ink-blackened hands on
a grubby towel. He had black hair covering every
inch of him except for a balding crown. I suppose he
was attractive in a Neanderthal way. There were
women—Bobbie was apparently one of them—who
thought a hairy back was the epitome of sexual at-
traction.

"Can I help you?" he asked, squinting a little as
if he sort of recognized me.

I smiled and handed him one of my cards. He
raised his dark eyebrows, then looked at me again,
and I swear his face turned pasty white. It was kind
of fun to watch.

"You're Herb Cooper, right?" I asked, enjoying
myself. It would be stupid of him to deny it because
his nametag said that he was indeed Herb Cooper.
Besides, I'd seen his hairy butt a few days ago, and

I suppose I could identify it again if Herb gave me any trouble.

He must have sensed that my question was rhetorical because he just nodded, suspicion hovering in his eyes. "You're that private detective Bobbie told me about. I got nothin' to say, so just get on out of here." His eyes darted around the room as if it had hidden microphones.

I pointedly glanced at his thick gold wedding band. "I was so hoping we could talk," I said in a sweet voice. "But I suppose I could call up your wife and ask her if she knew Edie—or Bobbie...."

He deflated like a balloon with a slow leak. "Okay, you got me. I just don't want this to get out, you understand. Marian would divorce me and take the kids away."

I've always wondered why people stray once they're married—do they know before uttering "I do" that they're likely to be unfaithful, or does it just happen? I try not to pass judgment, but I can't help wondering.

I assured him that I wasn't interested in talking to his wife if he answered a few of my questions. I wondered how he'd reacted the other day when the cops came calling. Probably was more helpful.

"Just met Bobbie a few months ago," Herb began, "at a bar. I was country line dancing with some woman—my wife was out of town—and I ended up with Bobbie during one of those mixers." So far, his story tallied with Bobbie's. Herb's face lit up at the memory. "Boy, she is somethin'. We got on like a house afire, and I got her phone number by the end of the evening. I called her up for a cup of coffee;

then one thing led to another...." He turned to me and had the grace to flush. "Well, you know how these things go."

I just nodded and asked another question. "Did you talk to Bobbie's roommate, Em, or her daughter, Edie, during your visits?"

He looked away. "I can't say that it was the first thing I thought about when I came to visit. But I've talked to Em a few times. She'd usually been drinking. And I talked to Edie once."

He wanted me to ask him, to gain some control of the interview, but I outwaited him. I don't know why control is so important to people in a situation like this, but I play the game as well as anyone.

He sighed and lowered his eyes to the counter. "She seemed nice enough. We just talked about, you know..."

I folded my arms and tipped my head to the side, enjoying his squirming. "No, what? Tell me."

His face went beet red and he was sweating. He wore a cologne that was nauseatingly sweet. Oooh, that was a turn on for me. I could see why Bobbie had the hots for this guy. Blecch. "Normal stuff like school."

I don't know why this guy bugged me. It wasn't just that he was unfaithful to his wife—hell, I didn't even know Marian. For all I knew, she was Attila the Hun with breasts.

"So let me get this straight," I said slowly. "You were in the living room and Edie came in and you talked about school. Did you mention your kids and how they liked school?" Okay, so it was a jab about his wandering eye. He deserved it.

There was a small silence. Herb's piggy eyes started roaming restlessly around the place, trying to find an escape route. "Oh, I dunno. Why does it matter?"

"What day and time was this?"

He thought hard, probably burning up a lot of brain cells because he even had to look up at the ceiling to find the answer. "Last Friday about four-thirty."

"And where were Bobbie's kids?"

Herb's neck seemed to bother him because he was moving his head around as if he was uncomfortable. "Oh, probably napping. Bobbie puts them down every day at the same time, okay?"

"That's interesting to know," I replied, "because I was there the other day at about that time, and you and Bobbie were going at it on the couch in the living room while the kids were watching *Power Rangers* on the tube."

He began to look for a way out again. "Okay, so they were probably doing the same thing," he said with resignation. "I'm not their parent, so it's none of my business."

We had gotten way off track, mostly because Herb just pissed me off. "Let's get back to the last time you saw Edie. Did she walk in on you two?"

He shook his head. "Bobbie worked an afternoon shift for another waitress who'd up and quit. So she was late getting back home. We only had a couple of hours together before she had to go back to work."

"So you talked to Edie about school and stuff. Was Rachel with her?"

He shook his head. "Rachel? I never met Rachel."

"Did Bobbie talk to Edie when she got home from work?"

Herb's smile was wry. "Bobbie was busy yelling at her kids."

Yeah, Mother of the Year.

FOURTEEN

I TRIED TO REACH Joe Blount at the number Bobbie had given me, but he wasn't there and no answering machine picked up. I drove over to the address, hoping to catch him at home.

Blount lived in a small weather-beaten house on Fernwood Place, across from Harry Della Russo Park in Revere. The yard was well maintained and included a small garden in the front. Someone had been doing some fall gardening because it looked as if someone had dug the garden up, planted some yew bushes, and spread fresh peat all around.

I pressed the buzzer, but no one answered. I left my business card in his door. As an afterthought, I left a note on the back of the card: "I'd like to talk to you about Edie Morris and Rachel McCarthy. Please call at your earliest convenience."

Mid-October in Boston can be a fickle time of year. You can get a really nice, warm day that reminds you of summer, then wake up the next day to cold, wind, and rain. Fortunately, Friday was a beautiful fall day, warm with a hint of coolness in the air, and the leaves were starting to turn from green to red, yellow, and orange.

One of the avenues I hadn't yet targeted was the runaway circuit. I had a friend who was the clearinghouse for all the halfway houses, soup kitchens, and day shelters in Boston. Mark Gianinni ran a

small, one-man operation called Runaway Alliance
out of his home office. He had volunteers from time
to time, usually runaways who were in transition
from the streets to a halfway house, but he was a
crusader who knew every facet of the system that
tried to help teens who lived on the streets.

Back in Eastie, I parked my Corsica and went up
to my apartment for lunch. Mark's line was busy, so
I heated up some canned soup, adding a couple of
fresh vegetables to make it taste almost homemade,
and sat down to eat.

At one o'clock, I took the subway to the Central
Square station in Cambridge. Mark lived a few
blocks from there, and if you knew only the general
direction in which he lived, you'd be able to guess
his building from the scads of kids hanging around
the stoop. I walked past them to the vestibule and
pressed Mark's buzzer. A young woman followed me
in. She had that dazed, unwashed look of someone
living on the streets. She wasn't much older than
Edie, and I wondered if Edie looked like that, or if
she was somewhere safe and warm and clean. I
doubted it.

"You here to see Mark?" the girl asked, eyeing
me suspiciously. I suppose I could have looked like
a case worker.

I nodded. I had only caught a glimpse of her eyes
before her stringy, dull brown hair fell over them.
She had that wounded, frightened-animal look. I was
glad she made no move to push her hair aside.

"You here looking for a kid?" It didn't take a
psychic to figure out why I was there, but I showed
her Edie's photo, anyway.

She shook her head to the unasked question and let me in to see Mark. As I walked down the hall to his open apartment door, I heard him talking on the phone. He had that politician's tone in his voice. Probably trying to wheedle money out of some Boston Brahmin.

"Of course, Mrs. Whittington. I certainly understand that Annabelle needs her asthma medication. And I know it's expensive." Mark was stretched out in a secondhand office chair that squeaked whenever he shifted his frame. "But if you could see your way clear to donate— Mmmm hmmm. Yes. I see. Well, that is very generous of you, Mrs. Whittington. I hope Annabelle is well. Yes, I will. Thank you again."

Mark's frizzy black hair fell in a tangled mass to his well-defined shoulders, and his crooked nose made his face more interesting than handsome. He'd always had a problem with his weight and kept off the pounds by eating almost a strictly vegetarian diet. But he had so much charisma and intensity that you couldn't take your eyes off him. When his blue eyes studied you with their laser beam intensity, your heart stopped for a moment, and you found yourself hoping that he approved of what he saw.

I watched as he put the phone down gently and muttered "Yes" softly. Then he saw me and stood up. "Hiya, Angie."

I threw my purse down and gave him a hug. "Trying to take the asthma medication away from her poor child, how dare you!" I chided.

"Dog, not child," he replied with a grin. "Her toy poodle can't breathe in this smog-ridden city."

"Why doesn't she just move?"

"Don't you know, darling?" Mark stood back and gestured into space, rolling his eyes heavenward and doing a fair imitation of the Brahmin accent. "This is the family homestead. My parents lived on Beacon Hill, and my grandparents, great-, and great-great-grandparents before them, and, well, I am descended from the Mayflower, you know."

I snorted. "She and every other Boston-born WASP."

"If they all had ancestors on the Mayflower," Mark added, throwing his hands up in the air, "the ship wouldn't have been able to leave the harbor in merry old England."

"It's like all those people who claim they attended Woodstock," I said.

Mark got down to business. "I know you're not here for a social call. What can I do for you?"

We had grown up together in Eastie, lived next door to each other. As a kid, Mark had been small and a little overweight. Consequently, he was always picked on by the neighborhood bullies. Mark and I had faced down the gangs more than once, and I'd gotten a few black eyes and bruised shins on his behalf.

When Mark was fifteen, he told his parents he was gay. They didn't take it well—especially his father, whose Italian machismo couldn't handle it. He had dragged Mark to the priest, hoping to talk some sense into him, but it didn't work.

Mark left home. I didn't hear from him for several days. I'd heard that Mr. Gianinni wouldn't allow Mark's name to be spoken in the house, but Mrs.

Gianinni had finally called me, and—in a hurried, whispered, tear-filled conversation—told me that Mark had been in touch and was living on the streets in the Combat Zone. She'd begged me and Ma to help him out.

Since Ma had always thought of Mark as her fourth son, we went down to the Zone on a frigid Friday night and found him huddled in the doorway of an adult movie theater. He lived with us until we graduated from high school, then went off to college.

The Runaway Alliance, which was a clearinghouse for homeless teens, was partly subsidized by various government agencies and wealthy do-gooders. To pay his rent, Mark published a popular magazine for Boston's music community—what was happening in rock, folk, alternative, blues, and jazz. Evidence of the latest issue sat in a corner of his living room. Blue-penciled, typeset galleys and photos spilled out over a six-foot table next to his desktop publishing system. A boy of about sixteen years old was working on the computer, word processing an article.

I explained the situation to Mark and showed him Edie's photo.

"Pretty girl," he said, studying it, "but there's a lot of sadness in her eyes."

I nodded. I had noticed that about Edie as well.

"I suppose you want me to ask around, see if anyone has seen her?"

"It would help," I replied.

He laid the photo down on his desk. "Doesn't sound too hard to do. I'll ask around for you."

"Sounds okay to me." I thanked him, and we

made plans to get together for lunch the following week.

From Cambridge, I headed over to Berkeley Street to see if Lee could get away for dinner. At the station, the desk sergeant at the lobby window buzzed me straight through the security doors. Lee Randolph is tall and thin with Art Garfunkel hair and thin, gold wire-rimmed glasses. He had a mustache when I first met him, but his most recent girlfriend convinced him to shave it off. Then she left him. But I thought he looked less like a college professor without the caterpillar over his lip. You'd never know it to look at him, but the guy was an ex-marine, and a Viet Nam vet, to boot.

Lee was waiting in his office. He'd been moved from a cubicle to a coveted office when he got a promotion and a raise a few months ago. He was gleefully rubbing his hands together when I walked in.

"Good to see you, Ange. Got a new place for us to try, a Greek restaurant."

I raised my eyebrows. "How much is this going to set me back, Champ?"

He shrugged, grinning as he moved papers around on his desk, shuffling through them in search, presumably, of the background checks I'd asked him to do. "Price of the background checks, babe."

I stepped forward and patted him on the back. "I appreciate your work, Lee. And I promise not to faint when the bill comes."

He grabbed his jacket and shoved some computer printouts at me. I had to practically break into a run to keep up with his long-legged stride. The restaurant

was only three blocks away, and there was an out-
door area if you wanted to sit on the sidewalk and
add a little smog to your meal to spice it up. We
opted for an indoor table.

Next to Italian food, Greek comes a close second
in my heart. I love the combination of flavors—the
lemon and nutmeg, olives and tomatoes, feta cheese
and spinach. I ordered the moussaka with a side of
rice pilaf, and Lee ordered the egg lemon soup and
spanikopita. Both of us ordered side Greek salads
with extra feta. One of the things Lee and I had in
common was a big appetite.

"Let's get ouzo," he said.

I gave him the look.

"What?" he complained.

"Booze before poker?" I asked. Some tortured
mandolinlike stringed instruments playing slow
Greek music came out of two small speakers above
us. Lee gave me a stern look over the tops of his
glasses. "What are you, my mother?"

I gave in.

The ouzos appeared in front of us as if by magic,
and Lee took a sip of his drink. "I've got a reunion
next weekend."

I was busy putting some ice from my water into
my ouzo.

"My unit reunion."

I stopped what I was doing. Oh. Viet Nam. Not
good.

"That should be fun," I said with a light tone.
Lee gave me a dark look. I put down my spoon and
leaned forward. "Is there anything that says you
have to go to it?"

"It's here in Boston at the Park Plaza. How am I going to get out of it?" He finished his ouzo and signaled the waiter.

I stopped him. "Come on, Lee. You want to be plastered before poker?"

He frowned. In the year that I had known Lee, he had become practically my best friend, next to my sisters, my childhood friend, Raina, and Mark. Because of our bond to the marine brotherhood, he knew things about me that I hadn't told anyone else. And I knew things about Lee that he'd never admit to anyone else.

One of the things I knew about Lee was that his mood could change from light to dark in the space of one minute. Sometimes I thought he might be manic-depressive, but he maintained a good front at work and in front of most people. It was a constant struggle for him to maintain the facade, but marines are trained to not show their feelings. Not to the general public.

Marines also don't like to be ordered around. I don't know how it happened, but Lee seemed to care what I thought of him. He didn't mind it when I played drill sergeant and told him what to do and what not to do. I found it kind of scary to have that much influence over someone, but I used it sparingly. And today, it was necessary.

Lee lowered his eyes and put the glass aside. A waiter approached our table. "Another, sir?"

Lee looked at me. I maintained steady, serious eye contact. "No, thanks. Make it iced tea," he finally said.

"Make that two," I said to the waiter, then turned

back to Lee. "You've got to stop letting this sort of shit get to you. Don't go. Don't see the guys who saved your ass in Da Nang. Keep all of this crap inside you and let it grow and take over your life. Christ, Lee, you're a grown man. This is the nineties. We're supposed to be in the age of taking responsibility for our actions."

He held up his hand. "Okay, enough's enough, Angie. You're right. I have to stop kvetching. Maybe it's the Jewish side of me." We grinned.

His father was the product of a Jewish-Catholic marriage; his mother, a Boston Brahmin atheist. Their marriage has lasted for forty-seven years. They live in Florida, and I'd met them a few months back when they came up to see their boy and visit the old neighborhood, Brookline. His dad kept telling him that I would be a perfect match for him. He kept asking me what I thought of his boy—his forty-four-year-old boy. His mother kept rolling her eyes and saying, "Sy, stop. You're embarrassing her."

At times, I wished that things were different for us and I could fall in love with Lee. The age difference wasn't it. Fifteen years difference wasn't all that bad. It was the fact that I wasn't ready to settle down.

Lee was looking for someone. He wanted to be married. His biological clock was ticking, and he wanted a kid more than anything else, even more than marriage.

And then, there were things I knew about Lee that even his buddies at work didn't know—things that I couldn't talk about. Ever.

"Do me a favor, Angie," he said after we had

devoured our salads. "You just have to think about it, okay?"

"Okay, what?"

"Come with me to the reunion."

I thought about it for a minute. I'd always been curious—what had the young Lee been like? "That could be dangerous, Lee."

"No, I could do this by myself," he protested. "I'd just like you to meet the guys."

I broke into a grin. "I meant it could be dangerous for you. I might learn something about you that you don't want me to know."

He looked thoughtful. "No, I think you know just about everything there is to know about me."

Our meals arrived and we tucked into them.

Lee was still working on his spinach pie while I scanned the printouts. I went right to the entry on Earlene's boyfriend. Stick's real name was Lance Mallory. Or Denny Fallon. Or Lyle Manning. Pick a name, any name.

"This is going to sound weird," Lee said after glancing at Stick's rap sheet, "but apparently we're not sure which of those is that guy's real name."

Great. "Why don't you know stuff like that?"

He shrugged. "It's not my department. Not my jurisdiction. Ask the Charlestown cops. Better still, don't."

No reflection on the cops in Charlestown, but it was a hard town to enforce the law when you couldn't get the eye witnesses to step forward to identify the criminals. Too many problems and not enough police to clean it up.

I imagine that finding out Stick's real name was

not top on their list of priorities. I read down the long list of arrests and bails. Mostly receiving stolen goods, a few possible burglaries, but the charges had always been dropped. Not a guy I planned to hang around too much. I had seen his friends, and I think I was lucky to get out of there with no more than a bruise across my shoulder blades.

Bobbie had been arrested for shoplifting five times and appeared in court three of those times. Twice the charges had been dropped.

Herb Cooper had a lot of unpaid parking tickets and a couple of DWIs. He was set to go to court on the first of November. His business was clean, and he didn't have any outstanding debts. Upstanding citizen stuff—until you got to the charge of molestation.

"Wa-ait a minute," I said. Lee was craning his neck over the table to see what I was so interested in.

"Oh, Cooper's charge of molestation?" He gestured with his fork. "You'll notice the charges were dropped."

"It would still be interesting to find out what that was all about. I've already talked to Herb, but another visit wouldn't be out of the question."

I went on to the next sheet. Joe Blount's record was also interesting. He'd been arrested for DWI several times, and once for exposing himself while intoxicated. It sounded like Blount had a drinking problem, just like half of the suspects in this case. The charges had been dropped in all cases.

There wasn't a whole lot that told me anything that would help me find Edie, but maybe I could turn over a few rocks and see what crawled out. I studied Herb Cooper's rap sheet, hoping to find the key to this dead-end case.

"The cops in Revere think he did it, too," Lee said, breaking into my thoughts.

"Who?"

"Cooper."

"Are they questioning him right now?"

Lee nodded. "They think he's a good candidate for both killing the McCarthy girl and for Edie's disappearance. Mac told me this morning that both Blount and Cooper agreed to a lie detector test." He shoveled a forkful of flaky phyllo pastry with spinach and feta filling into his mouth.

"What about Stick?"

Lee grinned. "He's made himself real scarce right now." He leaned over and gave me his this-is-privileged-information look. "Okay, you didn't hear this from me. Act surprised if and when Mac or Holmes tell you."

"Yeah, sure." I propped my elbow on the table and rested my chin on my hand, giving Lee my undivided attention. Lee grinned, knowing this was all bullshit. But at least he'd covered his ass.

"Blount is the only one who admits he saw Rachel alive on Friday, the day she disappeared."

"And Edie?"

"And Edie," he replied.

The waiter discreetly placed the check by Lee's elbow. I discreetly slid it over to my plate. Lee discreetly looked the other way.

FIFTEEN

FRIDAY NIGHT'S POKER GAME netted me about four dollars and fifty cents. Better than the last time—I'd lost nine dollars. We never played for high stakes, mostly because none of us could afford it, but also because it would take all the fun out of the game. Besides, we were all pretty bad at poker.

I woke up on Saturday morning and watched a couple of cartoons. I'm a cartoon addict and am partial to *The Tick* and *Animaniacs*. After a cup of coffee and a bagel, I washed up and dressed in a pair of jeans and a short-sleeved red blouse with a black vest. I was ready to see if Joe Blount would answer his door.

A dark-blue Ford pickup, about two or three years old, was parked in front of his house. I parked my car behind it. At his front door I could hear the television on—some sort of golf tournament with lots of hushes and restrained golf claps in between. I knocked and when no one answered, I knocked a little harder. Finally, I heard someone clomp over to the door. The door squeaked when it opened and a narrow face peered out of a narrow opening.

"Yes?" His eyes were red from sleep, and his hawk nose was speckled with broken blood vessels.

I introduced myself. He rubbed his hand over his face.

"Yes, I got your card last night. I meant to call

sometime today.'' He opened the door wider to let
me in. "This is as good a time as any.''

The living room was small and had that musty
smell that comes from never opening the windows
or vaccuuming very often. Blount stood there in a
pair of new blue jeans and a sleeveless T-shirt, the
kind my dad used to wear. He seemed aware of my
assessment and moved over to a chair to retrieve a
brown-and-white plaid sport shirt. As he was button-
ing it and tucking in the tails, I took time to study
him a little closer. He had large features—large eyes,
large chin, large lips. His dark hair was thin on top
and he combed it over in an effort to cover up what
was obvious.

He picked up a pair of brown loafers, and a tack
fell out of one shoe. Blount picked up the tack and
slipped it into his jeans pocket, then turned his attention back to me. "Can I get you anything,
Miss—?''

"Matelli,'' I repeated. "No, that's okay.'' I put
my shoulder bag down on the couch, a faded green,
purple, and brown flower fabric with patches of stuff-
ing coming out of the cushions. The dark-brown car-
pet was short and nubby like indoor/outdoor carpet-
ing, and the television was a small thirteen-inch set
with no cable outlet that I could see.

I tried to imagine Bobbie with this guy. On the
surface, Blount seemed to be a decent sort, and I
wondered why Bobbie had left him for Herb. Not
that Joe Blount was such a fabulous catch. Even with
the front door closed, I could hear the kids outside.
One kid in particular seemed to have a good set of
lungs on her.

Blount came back with a beer bottle in his hand. "Hope you don't mind," he said before taking a sip. I wondered if it was his first of the day. "So you're here to talk about Edie, right?"

"Yes, she's missing."

"I heard about that," he replied as he sat down on the couch near me.

"I suppose you heard it from the police?"

A greasy string from his comb-over detached itself and fell forward. He didn't seem to notice it. "Yeah, they said I was a suspect, but they can't prove anything. And I passed their damn test." He took a swig of beer from his bottle. "What d'you want to know?"

"How well did you know Edie?"

He grimaced. "Not well. She was Bobbie's roommate's kid. We said hi to each other. That's it."

"What about Rachel McCarthy?"

"Who?" He tried to look blank, but I didn't buy it. He saw that and changed his expression, as if light were dawning on him. "Oh, yeah. The dead girl. I only met her the once."

"When was that?" I asked.

"When I gave them a ride to the wall."

"Revere Beach?"

"Yeah," he said. He lifted the bottle to his lips, giving me the eye the whole time, as if he didn't trust me. As if challenging me to question his story. Yeah, I could see why he was one of Holmes and MacMillan's favorite suspects. The guy definitely had an attitude. The word "loser" came to mind.

I tried again. "When you dropped them off at the wall, did they tell you where they were going?"

"Nope."

"Did Edie seem upset?"

Blount shrugged, suddenly going noncommunicative on me. He looked restlessly around.

I tried another question, one that bothered me. "How did you happen to pick them up in the first place? I thought you weren't seeing Bobbie anymore."

I noticed sweat breaking out under his comb-over. It could have been from guilt, or it could have been because it was hot in his house. His eyes looked to a spot just beyond my shoulder as he said, "I saw them hitchhiking on Route One, and I picked them up. It's dangerous for young girls to be out there, even if there were two of them."

"They must have said something to you."

"Yeah," Blount replied, his chip firmly planted on his shoulder, "Edie said she was going back to her dad and Rachel was helping her get there. I tried to talk them out of it. When I couldn't, I let them off at the wall. I told them to think about it and call me if they changed their minds."

"Are you sure you haven't had contact with Edie since Friday?"

He slammed the half-full bottle down on the cheap particle board coffee table with more force than my question warranted. "What the hell kind of question is that? Are you trying to imply something?"

I smiled confidently, but inside, I didn't feel very confident. "Why, no, Joe. I don't know what you're talking about. You seem upset about something."

He ran his hand over his head, smearing the careful comb-over to the back of his head. "Well, with this one girl dead and the other missing, I guess I'm concerned.''

Blount was hiding something, but I wasn't going to find it out from him. His story about picking up the girls, then letting them off at the wall didn't ring true. The wall was hardly more than a few blocks from Edie's house. Besides, Blount didn't inspire confidence in me—I doubted he inspired enough confidence in Edie for her to confide that much in that short of a time.

I muttered a "Thank you for your time" as I stood up to leave.

He stood up as well, a little unsteadily, it appeared. "Is there any trace of Edie?" he asked.

I told him I was waiting to hear back from someone who had his finger on the pulse of the Boston runaway circuit.

"You think she's still around here?" he asked. "You know what I think? I think she decided not to go back to either parent. You know these young girls."

I shrugged. "Never hurts to search around. Thanks again for your time." I wondered what made him such an expert on young girls. He had kids, a son and a daughter, but he didn't strike me as the sensitive, understanding type of father.

As I headed out his door, he came after me. "Miss Matelli!" I turned around. "Will you let me know how it goes?"

I must have looked a little dubious because he added, "I feel responsible for those kids. If I'd just—" He fell silent.

I wondered if this was an act or if he really felt that way. I assured him I'd let him know—yeah, the way I'd make reports to Earlene about my progress on finding Edie.

SIXTEEN

I DROVE BY Herb Cooper's shop, hoping to catch him there. I wanted to talk to him without dragging his wife into it, if it was possible, but I wasn't above stopping at his house and asking a few questions. Fortunately, his pickup was out front, and the door was open, which meant he was in, although the Closed sign was hanging on the door.

"Hey, we're closed," Herb said as he stepped through the door to the back room. When he saw me, his face fell. "Oh, it's you."

"Hey, that's no way to greet a potential customer."

"Potential troublemaker, more likely," he grumbled, resting his hands on the counter between us. "What do you want?"

"I have a couple more questions."

He pushed away from the counter, crossed his arms, and leaned up against the wall. "Make it quick. I got a date."

I told him what I found out about his past, the molestation charge that had been dropped.

He looked troubled and angry. "Yeah, I remember that. It was one of our babysitters. She got a little friendly with me, and when I didn't return her affection, she got mad and called the cops."

Well, that was his side of the story. I didn't consider the matter closed, but I like to think I can reserve judgment on scum-sucking bastards who like underage girls. "Are you sure you didn't lead her on a bit, or maybe liked her just a little?"

Cooper's brow darkened and he pushed away from the wall, his hands becoming fists. "What're you trying to say?"

I kept a good distance between us, and held up my hands. "I'm just curious what her side of it is."

His brow darkened. "Fine. Go ask her."

"What's her name?"

"You're not gettin' it from me," he said, walking to the door and opening it for me. "Get the hell out."

As I drove away, he was standing at the door, watching to make sure I was leaving.

On a whim, I stopped at a little Italian bakery in Day Square called Angelina's and picked up about two dozen cookies and a few biscotti and other bakery items. I figured my niece and nephew might stop by, and if they didn't, I could take the whole batch to Ma's on Sunday. If I didn't eat it all first.

When I got home, I called the office—I had two messages. One was from Joe Blount, asking if I'd found Edie yet. I thought it was awfully presumptuous of him to call so soon after I'd talked to him. What, he thought I just had to look under a rug and Edie would be there?

The other message was from Detective Holmes asking me to call him either at the office or at home. He left both numbers. I ignored Blount's call but tried to reach Detective Holmes at the office. The sergeant who answered told me that he'd gone for the day. I tried his home number and got his answering machine. I didn't realize until then that he

had a nice voice. I'd been too busy with reporting
Edie as a missing person to notice how deep and
resonant it was. I left a message for him to call when
he got in.

As soon as I hung up, the phone rang. It was Ev.

"I'm tired of sitting in the Parker House lounge
every day after work," he said. Ev had told me that
he'd gotten a temporary transfer to Tremont Street
marine recruiting office across from the Common until Edie was found. "I want to do something different, anything."

"Come on over," I said. I was tired and could
have used a good night's rest, but Ev and I hadn't
connected much during my investigation.

I brewed some coffee, took out the biscotti and
other cookies I'd bought, and found a bottle of red
table wine. If Ev was the same guy I'd known a few
years ago, I didn't think I'd be opening the wine, but
I like to be prepared.

There was a knock at the door and when I opened
it, Ev stood there. He wore chinos and a long-
sleeved, blue-and-green-striped polo shirt with a
white collar, the uniform of the military man when
he wanted to go civilian. I don't know what it is
about being in the military, but you suddenly lose all
sense of your own style. When you live on base and
most of the people you're in contact with are all
wearing the same drab khaki or olive-green uniforms,
you forget what the outside world is like and fashion
trends pass you by. So when you have to buy civvies,
you go for that classic outdoorsy look so you don't
have to buy too many civilian clothes to keep up with
the fast-paced outside world. We all look like we

stepped out of a Land's End or Eddie Bauer catalogue.

"Nice place," he said as he stepped inside and surveyed my spartan living room. He was probably just being polite. We're not talking Ethan Allan here. I was still practically living out of boxes. Most of the furniture was secondhand and none of it really went together. I had, however, in a moment of insanity, painted the entire apartment myself. The living room was a cool blue, my kitchen was yellow and white, and my two bedrooms had been respectively painted a mint green and the same blue as the living room. My bathroom was the only room I hadn't taken a brush to. I'd run out of steam by then, so it remained an awful shade of pink.

Ev accepted my offer of coffee, and I went back in the kitchen to pour two mugs and bring out the cookies.

"You make these?" Ev asked as he bit into his second cookie.

"I suppose I could be coy and say yes, but the truth of the matter is that they come from the bakery around the corner." I stretched out on my easy chair, watching Ev. He looked relaxed enough, if you didn't know any better. "So what's really up, Ev?"

He sipped his brew. "Detective Holmes called today. Said he's done interviewing and you can get on with your investigating."

I thought the interviews had gone pretty fast. That must be why Holmes had tried to reach me today. I told Ev what I'd learned today, trying to give him an accurate report of my conversations with Blount, Cooper, and Stick over the past few days. Some of it was going over familiar territory, stuff I'd already told him, but I needed to talk to someone, and he was handy. Sounding it out with him in the room made it clearer for me.

When I was done, Ev stared into his coffee. "So you think you'll find Edie soon?"

"I hope so. I get more afraid for her welfare with each day she's still missing." I realized we hadn't talked much about Edie. I'd seen her room at Earlene's house and got something of a sense of her. "What's Edie like these days? Tell me something about her interests."

Ev gave me a curious look, then nodded. "Edie's a good kid. She likes to play soccer—was getting pretty good at it, too. She was thinking about going out for the girls' soccer team when she got into high school this year. She likes to dance and I hate her taste in music, that 'rap crap,' as I call it."

We smiled knowingly. Our parents had hated our music, and now Ev was in his parents' situation. I didn't relish the thought of being the parent of a teenager, but I supposed it would happen someday.

"She's told me she wants to be a doctor," he continued. "But then, she'll also tell me she wants to go into modern dance. I think she may end up in the marines for a few years. Like her dad."

"So she sounds like a nice kid," I said. "Still, it must have been hard on her to go through so many moves with you."

Ev gave me a rueful smile. "I've been thinking of leaving the marines next year, settling down until Edie finishes high school. She's had some temper outbursts over small things, and she wasn't thrilled when I told her she couldn't start dating until she turned sixteen.''

I thought about Michael and Stephanie and their irresponsible mother. Even though Sophia hadn't provided the most stable environment for them, Ma and Rosa and I had been there for them. I wondered if Stephanie, who was now ten, would think of running away when she became a teenager. Or Michael. I loved my other nieces and nephews, too, but I'd been there when Michael and Stephanie were born. Although I'd been in the military for a lot of the time they were growing up, I'd grown close to them over the last year.

''What was the last day like,'' I asked, ''the last day you spent with Edie?''

Ev stared at a speck on the wall behind my shoulder. ''The morning that she disappeared, we'd had another fight. She liked this boy at school and he'd asked her out. I told her no. I'd seen the boy—he had a nose ring, for God's sake.'' He suddenly shifted back his focus, and changed the subject. ''Do you think Joe Blount knows more than he's telling you?''

''It's just a feeling, nothing he said in particular,'' I replied, realizing how vague that sounded. Now I questioned my reasoning. Blount had a record of drunk driving, and he'd had the opportunity—but he practically told us he was guilty by admitting that he'd given the girls a ride on Friday afternoon. Still, it bothered me a little. It was too pat. Why would someone want to implicate himself for these crimes? I brushed my misgivings aside.

''You know, I think it became clear to me when

I asked Blount if he had seen the girls after leaving them at the wall. He just seemed to get nervous. He became abrupt with me and seemed to want to end the interview quickly.''

Ev looked thoughtful. ''I'll talk to Detective Holmes, ask him if he can let me see a copy of the polygraph tests on both suspects and the questions asked.''

I nodded. It would give him something to do, make him feel useful. And he had more pull than I did. I don't know why—the military and the civilian police didn't have an awful lot in common—but I didn't question it.

Police almost never let PIs interfere with an ongoing case, yet because Ev had talked to MacMillan and Holmes, they were letting me walk all over this case. Ev must have noted the frown on my face.

''What's up?''

I hesitated. It was clear to me that Ev had a ''sensitive'' job. Then I decided to ask anyway. ''Why are the police being so cooperative with you? It's one thing to walk into the station in your B uniform to impress them into taking your case seriously. I think the uniform works to your advantage because a lot of cops were once in the military. But you seem to have a lot of pull with them on the investigation.''

Ev shrugged. ''I know some people in Washington,'' was all he said. I left it at that. I had a feeling Ev and his ''people'' put on the pressure.

Ev spoke again. ''Angie, I want to thank you for what you said to me the other day.''

I felt my face flush. I thought I'd sounded harsh. ''I didn't have any right to speak to you like that.''

He shook his head. "It's what I needed. You know us old marines. Never say die." We both chuckled weakly.

We sat in companionable silence, munching bakery cookies and sipping coffee.

Ev broke the quiet. "I miss her so much. Do you think there's any chance she's still alive?" He blinked several times, as close as I'd ever seen him come to tears. I averted my eyes, drew my knees up, and hugged them. This sort of nurturing wasn't my strength. I was more comfortable with making dinner for a troubled person, nourishing the body rather than the soul. Besides, Ev wouldn't be comfortable if I tried to play pop psychologist.

I was careful choosing my words. "Rachel's body was found on Revere Beach, but Edie's wasn't."

Ev leaned toward me. He had control of himself again, but was now as intense as I've ever seen him. "But why hasn't she gone to the police or gotten to a phone?"

Good question. I ran over the facts in my mind, trying different scenarios on for size. "Maybe she was threatened, warned that if she told anyone that she witnessed Rachel's death, her loved ones would be harmed. Maybe she thinks it's best not to come forward because of that. Maybe she has amnesia."

I thought of another possibility for why Edie hadn't come forward yet, but I didn't say it out loud.

Ev said it for me. "There are two other possibilities that you haven't mentioned." I stayed silent, blinking back tears of my own. "She can't get to me because someone's holding her captive or she's dead.'' His voice sounded rough on the last two words.

I put my hand on his arm. A beat passed; then Ev looked into my eyes. I could feel the electricity pass between us and, God help me, I couldn't stop myself. I leaned over for the kiss that was inevitable. It must have lasted only a few seconds, but it seemed like an eternity. When I pulled back, I was thinking, What the hell do I think I'm doing? And when I looked at him, I could tell that he was thinking the same thing. Yeah, I can be a Mensa member sometimes.

I took a deep breath. ''Oh, boy'' were my first words.

Ev grinned, then began to chuckle. The tension passed. I shook my head; he ran his hand through his short, blond hair and down the back of his neck.

''Sorry about that, Chief,'' were my next words.

Ev sobered up long enough to give me that sexy half-grin he used to throw at me back in the old days. ''That was nice, Angie. Don't apologize for something we both wanted.''

Although I tried for the somber look, a smile tugged at my mouth. ''But this isn't the right time, is it?''

Before he could answer me, I picked up our empty coffee mugs and went into the kitchen, as much for refills as for the chance to pull myself together.

It hadn't been an easy year for me. I'd left military service, bought an apartment building in my old neighborhood, launched my private investigation business, and had no love life to speak of. Ma was more than happy to set me up, and in fact had made several overtures in that direction—''Angie, you remember my best friend, Martha, don't you? Well, her son is a podiatrist and he's single!''—but I'd managed to avoid her clutches up to now.

Ev was the first available man I was attracted to in that time and I'd probably just screwed up my chances of anything coming of this. A drop of hot coffee splashed, stinging my wrist. I jumped, set the pot down, shook my hand, and cursed.

"Everything all right in there?" Ev called from the living room.

"Just fine," I replied sweetly. I ran cold water over my hand and felt guilt wash over me as well. What an incredibly selfish bitch I was. Here was a guy who was worried about his little girl, and I'm drooling over him like a starving woman over a piece of filet mignon. I should be concentrating on finding Edie.

After mentally kicking myself for about a minute, I took a deep breath, plastered a smile across my face, and brought the coffee back into the living room.

"Hey, Angie, remember when that obnoxious corporal was transferred into our unit?"

I chuckled, remembering some of the pranks we pulled. Ev and I had been more than major and sergeant, less than lovers. We had loved playing practical jokes on unsuspecting, humor-impaired comms, and poking cruel fun at the inanities of military life.

"Yeah, he was a real pain to be around," I recalled, "always double-checking and triple-checking his work and everyone else's work around him." He'd made our lives a misery because he was a prissy little anal retentive asshole who reveled in paperwork.

"Think he ever found out who put the chicken carcass in his air vent?" I had flirted with the corporal back at the office while Ev sneaked into the guy's room, unscrewed the grillwork to the air vent, and slipped the chicken carcass into it. For weeks, the stench grew stronger as the corporal spent hours cleaning his room with Lysol and ammonia, trying to find the souce of the stink. Finally, the big day came for inspection. The captain came by, screwed up her nose, and demanded to know where the reek was coming from.

"He had tears in his eyes while she yelled at him," I said, gasping for air between sobs of laughter. Ev clapped a hand over half of his face, which was fast becoming a bright shade of red.

"I had to hold my breath to keep from laughing," he said.

When we had calmed down, Ev stood up to go. "I'm keeping you up," he said.

"Hey, that's my line," I returned with a grin. He made a fist and chucked me on the shoulder just before he left. I promised him that tomorrow, I'd give him a report on my investigation so far.

I WAS GETTING ready for bed when the phone rang.

"This is Robert Holmes returning your call," said the deep and pleasant voice on the other end. "I hope I'm not calling too late."

"No, not at all." In fact, I suddenly found that I was wide awake. "You called me earlier."

"Yes, I did. I wanted to tell you that, unofficially, you are welcome to continue your investigation."

"Thanks," I replied, "I appreciate that." I wasn't sure how far I could go with this guy. I mean, was he going to give me information without a fight, or was he going to play close to the vest? So I thought I'd step past the barriers erected to keep nosy private eyes out of police business and see where it got me. "So, tell me, who did you interview?"

There was a pause. "Can you meet me for coffee now?" His question caught me off guard enough that I agreed, and we decided on a little coffee shop on Route 1 in Everett.

Shari's Place was housed in an old trucker's diner, and very little had been done to fix it up. The cracked black-and-red checkered linoleum was still there, as was the not-so-shiny chrome-and-formica counter. The only thing Shari had done to brighten up the place was to hang bright dancing-vegetable curtains in the plate-glass windows and change the music on the jukebox to '60s Motown and pop classics.

I waited for Holmes, cradling a thick china mug filled with fairly good coffee. It was hot and black and rich for a change. Most diner coffee barely qualified as muddy water, let alone real coffee. I sipped it and watched for him.

I almost didn't recognize him when he walked in because he was out of uniform. He wore a faded red short-sleeved polo shirt and jeans that hugged his legs and trim waist. He obviously worked out, and the effect was very nice.

When he slipped into the booth, the waitress must

have known him because she brought his coffee over immediately.

"You want anything else, sugar?" she asked, eyeing me speculatively, but addressing the question to him. She was in her midtwenties and very pretty in a Lena Horne sort of way.

"They make a great rhubarb pie here," he told me. I nodded, feeling a little out of place in a non-Italian, all-American, apple-pie diner.

"Sounds good," I replied, not sure if I'd like rhubarb or not. It was one of the few vegetables and fruits I hadn't tried. But I'll try anything once.

"Two rhubarbs with ice cream, Lakeisha," he told her. The waitress turned to leave, giving Holmes one more smoldering look that he seemed totally unaware of.

"Okay, what was so important that you couldn't tell me over the phone?" I asked as I looked into my almost empty coffee mug. As if by magic, the waitress reappeared with two large slabs of pie and ice cream, and a refill for me. She glided away just as silently.

"I thought we could have a little casual conversation," he said, being maddeningly evasive. "Maybe you could tell me how your investigation is going and I could give you an idea of how things are going in the department."

Okay, two can play that game. "Oh, so you want to talk about the case. But which case? The two seem to be connected, and I understand that you and MacMillan have joined forces."

He nodded imperceptibly. "Officially, as of this

afternoon. There are several factors that indicate that the two cases may be connected—"

"Oh, cut the bullshit, Rob," I finally said. I hate that kind of slippery talk. That's part of the reason I got out of the military. I got tired of having to play their games and try to read between the "military speak" whenever I got a memo from my superiors.

I gave him a rundown of my interviews with Cooper and Blount, and what I thought of them. Then, for my own benefit as much as Holmes', I ticked off the things that were known about the linked cases. "We both know that Rachel and Edie were best friends, two lonely kids at a new school who latched on to each other. Edie was unhappy with Mom and started to suspect that she wasn't telling the truth about Dad. She confided in Rachel and—What? Rachel agreed to help? But how? Did she run away with Edie to help her find her dad? How could she leave parents who obviously loved her?"

"It seems the most likely scenario," Holmes said thoughtfully. He ate some of his pie and sipped his coffee.

"What was your take on Earlene?"

He frowned in a pensive manner. "She struck me as self-absorbed, more worried about whether we thought she was a bad mother than where her daughter was and if she was alive. She's also a substance abuser."

"I was wondering what you thought about the possibility of Earlene hiding her daughter from Ev."

Holmes's expression remained impassive, but the glint in his eyes told me he was interested. "Hypothetically speaking, how would she do this? How would she know that the father would find them?''

I'd thought about that one already. ''Remember that Edie called him from a Lechmere pay phone a few weeks ago, then hung up abruptly. Suppose that Earlene was there shopping, and caught Edie on the phone. She realizes that Ev will find them. She finds a place to take Edie.''

''But why wouldn't she just get up and leave the area? She doesn't really have anything holding her here.'' Holmes seemed to enjoy playing devil's advocate. He started ticking items off on his fingers. ''A low-paying clerical job, a house shared with another woman and her kids, no family, no friends. Why not just run?''

I shrugged, realizing that my theory did seem kind of weak. ''Maybe she was tired of running. Maybe her boyfriend keeps her here.''

Holmes rolled his eyes. ''Have you met him?''

I smiled and nodded. ''Love is blind.''

''And deaf and dumb,'' he added. We laughed, but I could see he was going to take my suggestion seriously.

''Herb,'' was all I said.

Holmes shook his head, smiling. ''Scared to death his wife'll find out.''

''The dreaded Marian. Tell me about the dropped charge of sexual molestation.''

Holmes shrugged. ''The girl was underage—a babysitter, I believe. We talked to her, and now she swears he didn't do it and she was just young and impressionable. He's still on our list of suspects, although he passed the polygraph today.''

"Have you been able to uncover anything else about him?" I asked.

"The only other thing in his background that we uncovered was that he has a condo that his wife doesn't know about," Holmes said. "I have a feeling it's for those afternoon meetings with Bobbie."

I nodded absently, half-listening. "Why are you really doing this, Rob?" I asked, changing the subject. It wasn't that I wasn't grateful, and he did sort of answer my question earlier, but it didn't sit right—cops didn't just give up information this easily without wanting something more back. "Does Ev have that much pull in Washington?"

He grinned. "Well, I have to say the guy has friends in high places, but I haven't exactly been unwilling to work with you."

"Why?"

His smile disappeared and something in his face closed down. "Let's just say that I have a personal interest."

"Someone in your family disappeared," I blurted out. He jerked back as if I'd shot him. Sometimes I can be insensitive when people don't want to talk about something.

When he finally looked up at me, there was a dangerous glint in his eyes. "My younger sister, Josephine. I was twelve and she was eight. One day, Josie just didn't come home from school. We went searching and didn't find the body for four days." I suddenly wished I hadn't been so curious. But he seemed to need to talk about it. His face tightened with anger. "She'd been molested and thrown into a trash bin. We never caught the monster who did it, but we had our suspicions."

Boy, there wasn't much to say to that. "I'm sorry. That's why you work in Missing Persons now?"

"I used to be a private investigator like you, specializing in missing children, but by the time most of the cases came to me, the leads were cold and the children dead." He had pushed away his half-finished pie and sipped his coffee. "So I decided to try it from the other side. The police weren't very cooperative when I was a PI, so I make an effort to help private investigators whenever they're working on one of my cases. In my opinion, the more help, the better. There's no ego here when it comes to a missing or dead child."

"So you're working from the inside now." It was a fascinating glimpse into what made one cop tick, but I wanted to get back to Edie and Rachel. Holmes seemed to sense that and he became more business-like. I wanted him to reveal whatever he knew about Joe Blount, without letting him know what I already knew. I guess I still play those kinds of bullshit games when I have to, but Holmes hadn't been real forthcoming about what he knew, and I hadn't been real generous, either. In a way, this was a meeting meant to gather information on both sides.

"So have you found anyone who saw Edie and Rachel together on Friday?" Not the most subtle way to get the information I wanted, but it was effective. Besides, he probably already suspected that Lee had told me.

"The biggest problem we've had up until now is

that no one has come forward to acknowledge that they saw the two girls together.''

I prompted him. ''You said up until now.''

Holmes had the grace to not roll his eyes at my obvious attempt to suck information out of him. ''Joe Blount was the last person to admit seeing the two girls on Friday afternoon after school.''

I shook my head. ''Did he admit to anything else?''

A dark look passed over his face. ''No. He said he gave them a ride to the wall and dropped them off.''

''Sounds like you don't believe him.'' I wasn't sure I did, either. But then again, I wasn't sure how much of Bobbie and Herb's story I believed. Maybe Herb did see Edie and Rachel talking to Blount, but did he really see them get in Blount's car and drive off? And Bobbie had been awfully quick to become Herb's alibi.

''It's not out of the realm of possibility. Edie wanted to get home, she had no money, and God knows her mother didn't have any, either. Hitching would be the only way,'' he reasoned.

''Not the smartest thing to do for either a fourteen-year-old girl or anyone else,'' I said. ''And she did have someone—her father—who would have been glad to pay for a plane ticket.''

Holmes picked at the crust of his pie. ''Blount took a polygraph test this morning, too.''

''What, he didn't pass?''

''Oh, he passed, all right. The fucker passed with flying colors. Problem is—''

I finished his sentence for him. "He's still on the Column A suspect list, just like Cooper."

He drummed his fingers on the tabletop, a habit I always found annoying. "It all fits. He had the opportunity, a past that gives him a motive." He pushed back from the table, sprawling his compact frame in the booth.

"But you like Cooper for this murder," I said.

"Call it a gut feeling."

"What about Blount, don't you think he could have done it?" I asked.

"Hey, it sounds like you're defending Cooper."

"Just playing devil's advocate." But I understood his reasoning. When I was a criminal investigator in the marines, there were many times I interviewed a dozen suspects for a crime, and any one of them could have done it. But there'd be something about one of them—maybe a bit too cocky, a bit too nervous, or just having too pat an alibi. I would just know that was our boy.

I thought back to this afternoon. There was just something wrong about the way both Cooper and Blount answered my questions, as if they'd been prepared. Of course, they'd both had a polygraph, and my questions probably weren't far removed from what they'd been asked during the test. Except for my last question to Blount, the question about if he'd seen the girls later after leaving the wall—he'd seemed unprepared for that one. But he'd passed that damn test.

Holmes was still talking and I tuned in again. "Between us, Mac and I have interviewed almost two dozen people about Rachel and Edie. Once the two missing girls were connected, we went back and interviewed the suspects in Rachel's case and came up empty. None of them could be linked to Edie, as well. Besides Earlene Morrow and her roommate, the three men are the only other suspects." He looked at me from under furrowed brows.

"What about Stick? Why have you eliminated him?" I had my own reasons, but I wanted to hear Holmes's reasons.

"He may have a rap sheet, but he doesn't have the sort of past Cooper and Blount have. And considering the fact that he allegedly works in stolen goods, I think Stick's too smart to thumb his nose at the law when it comes to underage girls and murder."

"You should give Earlene a polygraph."

"She wouldn't consent to one. Told us to go to hell. It's her little girl who's missing, so fuck off."

"Well, we do know that polygraphs are only about seventy percent accurate anyway."

He shook his head. "Yeah, I know. That's why I searched both Cooper and Blount's trash last night."

I mentally kicked myself for not thinking of that. It wasn't the most pleasant job in the world, but it was effective. You can learn almost anything you want to know by looking in someone's garbage. "So did you find out anything?"

Holmes smirked. "That Blount eats a lot of TV dinners and take-out. He prefers Healthy Choice to Swanson's, deli to pizza, he uses Trojans extra sensitive, and wears briefs. Typical divorced guy stuff. Cooper's trash is pretty much what you'd expect of a divorced man. No child porn, nothing out of the ordinary.''

I persisted. ''There must be more to your gut feeling than that.''

He pushed his coffee mug away. ''In Blount's trash, there were an awful lot of deli wrappers and TV dinner boxes for one week's worth of garbage. But that's not enough to go on. His kids come to visit every other weekend. Without more proof, we can't get a search warrant to his house.''

''What kind of questions did you ask them on the test?''

''The usual. Was Friday the last time you saw Rachel and Edie? Did you kill Rachel McCarthy? Both men answered those questions without even breaking a sweat.''

I had a thought. ''Listen, Ev Morrow will be asking for a copy of the test results and the questions. Can you get me a copy as well?'' I'd had some experience with polygraphs, and one thing I'd learned was that the wrong question could produce the wrong result.

''Sure.'' Holmes seemed a little annoyed, as if I were questioning how he did his job. I decided to explain.

''When I was in the marines, we had a soldier who was suspected of being the mule in a drug connection between Thailand and San Diego,'' I said. ''He almost got away with it because of the way a question was phrased—he was asked if he had ever taken drugs out of Thailand. Since he picked up the drugs in Guam and took them to the States, it wasn't a relevant question. If one of the interrogators hadn't spotted the flaw in the questioning and ordered another polygraph, he wouldn't have been implicated.''

Holmes slowly nodded his understanding. ''So you think maybe the right questions weren't asked.''

I shrugged. ''It was early in the investigation and you didn't have all the facts. And then there was the question I asked Blount that got the most response.'' I repeated the question I'd asked Blount, about the last time he'd seen Edie. ''He seemed surprised and angry that I would ask that question.''

Holmes frowned as if trying to recall something. ''I don't think we asked that,'' he finally admitted. ''It's worth getting him back in for another test.''

''If he agrees to another one.'' The chances of that weren't great. Any good lawyer would tell his client that he took one polygraph and didn't need to take another.

We were silent for a moment, both lost in our thoughts.

Holmes's next words sounded desolate and desperate. ''I just know he was lying about something, but we've got nothing.''

I had been thinking while Holmes was venting. Now I gave him an enigmatic look. ''But maybe I can come up with something for you.''

He was careful not to look excited. At least, I think that's what he was doing. In fact, he was studying the melting ice cream on his pie plate as if he were on a whale watch. ''Of course, I have no control over what you do from here on, Angela. You aren't working under the same restrictions I am.'' He gave me a significant look. ''Of course, I expect that whatever you find, you'll turn over to me.''

Of course.

SEVENTEEN

AFTER ROB HOLMES LEFT, I stayed at the diner, taking notes on the back of the rhubarb-stained paper placemat of our conversation and trying to get caught up on a case that had gotten away from me. I felt as if I were trying to put the pieces of several jigsaw puzzles together into a coherent picture. Reviewing the information on paper didn't make anything click, but it seemed that no one I'd interviewed so far was even remotely a possibility, with the exception of Joe Blount and Herb Cooper.

Okay, Stick was, but only because he was this enigmatic character. But unofficially, I'd eliminated Stick. He wouldn't risk his illegal activities for his girlfriend's daughter, someone he'd known for less than six months.

And Bobbie—if she couldn't pay attention to her own kids, how would she find the attention span to murder one child and make another disappear into thin air?

Earlene, well, she was still on my suspect list, but Holmes had ticked off some good points in her favor. She could have run away easily, but had stayed.

Herb Cooper might appear to be just a blustery goof with nothing more sinister in his background than a couple of DWIs, a secret condo, and a mistress, but there was still the matter of allegedly molesting a minor, even if the charge had been eventually dropped.

I also got the feeling that both Cooper and Bobbie were hiding something else. I'm not sure it was something that related to the case at hand, but I had to find out. I decided to go over to the depressing little house where Bobbie and Earlene lived, just one more time.

BOBBIE WAS HOME, getting ready for work. She was lacquering her hair into place, probably to protect it from all the grease in that joint. I didn't see Herb around, and I didn't ask. She wasn't pleased to see me.

"Em's out with Stick. I think they went to New Hampshire with some of Stick's biker friends."

I guess I was disappointed that Earlene would leave the state while her daughter was missing, but I really wasn't all that surprised. For a moment I panicked, wondering if she was going to get Edie from some hiding place and take off with her. But then I thought of Stick and decided he was much too savvy to get involved in a case of child abduction, not with his record and the police on his case every moment.

"Actually, I wanted to talk to you again."

Bobbie grabbed her purse and threw her lipstick and compact into it without looking at me. "I've told you everything I know," she said in a weary tone.

"Not quite," I replied, hoping I could pull this off. I sat in an easy chair, the kind that had been popular back in the late seventies. It squeaked when I tried to find the least uncomfortable position.

Bobbie stopped and looked up at me, her face slowly turning white under her makeup.

"Herb told me the rest."

She closed her eyes and bit her lip. "That didn't have anything to do with Edie and Rachel."

"Tell me your side of it."

She gave me a suspicious look, then shrugged and sat down on the couch. "Look, I guess I should have told Joe outright that I wasn't going to see him anymore, but I thought he'd get the message when I started breaking dates with him. But no, he had to come by when Herb was here."

"What time was this?" I asked.

"About five. Herb and I were"—she looked coyly at me—"well, we were getting dressed, and Joe knocked on my bedroom door. I opened it, thinking it was Em or one of the kids. He sees me, looks at Herb, and gets really mad. His face gets all flushed and the look in his eyes scares me."

She took out a Kool and lit it. "I could tell he'd been drinking—it was never hard to tell with Joe. His nose gets red and his eyes get bloodshot. I guess that's why his wife threw him out."

I knew he was divorced and had kids, but I hadn't known his wife was the one who had filed for divorce. Some PI—I'd gotten information on their run-ins with the law, but I hadn't gathered a full background on any of my suspects. I filed that away and got back to the subject at hand. "So Joe came in unexpectedly and met Herb. What did you and Herb do?"

"I just said, 'Oh, hello, Joe.' Herb stepped in front

of me and took Joe's elbow and helped him out the door.''

I thought about asking Bobbie if she knew about the dropped charge of sexual molestation of an underaged girl. But it didn't seem to serve any purpose. Bobbie hadn't known Herb back then. ''Do you know if Herb saw Edie or Rachel in the house as he was helping Joe leave?''

Bobbie narrowed her eyes and expelled the minty smoke. ''I thought you said Herb already told you this story.''

I shrugged. ''I stretched the truth a little.''

''I won't tell this to any cop,'' she said, getting up and pacing, one hand clasping the elbow of the other arm. ''I'll deny everything if anyone else comes to question me.''

''I don't understand. Why? What does it matter?''

Bobbie turned to look at me. ''Because of Herb's wife.''

I was mystified. ''You want to keep this from his wife? Don't you want Herb all to yourself?''

Bobbie stubbed out her cigarette, grinding it into the ashtray until gold and brown tobacco flakes spilled out of the butt. She sat back down on the couch. ''I'm not interested in marriage or in a relationship. I just want a good time, a man to pay for my dinner, buy me things. Herb's good to me; then he goes home to the wife and kids.''

I thought that was kind of a sad way to go through life, but it wasn't my decision. ''Look, all I want to do is find Edie. I'm not interested in making things difficult for you and Herb. As far as I'm concerned, that's your af—business. But I would like some cooperation from you. I promise you won't have to talk to the cops."

Bobbie was silent for a minute, watching me as if she were assessing how honest I was. Then she seemed to make a decision because she got up again and went over to the phone on a table on the far side of the room. The handset was grubby with fingerprints and dried-on food. She didn't seem to notice.

She punched in a number and waited. "Herb? I need to see you now." She waited. "You're not too busy, right? Okay. Fifteen minutes." She hung up.

We waited, and about ten minutes passed before we heard his car door slam. He was three minutes early, probably anticipating a little whoopee session before going home to the wife.

His face fell when Bobbie let him in and he laid eyes on me. Bobbie was halfway through another Kool.

He eyed me warily while he moved over to her and slipped his arm around her waist. "What's goin' on, babe? This one bugging you?"

Bobbie kissed him and led him back to the couch, explaining things to him.

"I still don't trust her," he muttered darkly while she patted his hand.

I took over. "Look, Herb. I don't mean to make trouble for you, but a girl's life may be at stake here. You got kids?"

He thought about that one as if I had some hidden meaning in that question. "Yeah, three," he grudgingly admitted. "Two boys and a girl."

"How would you feel if your daughter were missing? Wouldn't you want everyone who had any connection with a suspect to come forward and tell what they saw?''

He closed his eyes and let out a deep sigh. "Yeah. I guess." With enthusiasm like that, we're talking Father of the Year here.

"So tell her what you saw last Friday when you booted Joe out of the house," Bobbie said. She looked at her watch, anxious to get to work.

Herb looked at me. "Edie and Rachel were coming up the walk when Joe was going to his car. He stopped and looked back at the house once. Edie stopped and talked to him. He didn't seem to notice her at first, but then he looked down at her and Rachel."

I remembered our last conversation. "Wait a minute. You told me you never met Rachel."

He shifted in his seat. Bobbie squeezed his hand. "Look, I read the papers, all right?" he said a little impatiently. "I saw the photo of her. I recognized the girl with Edie as this Rachel, okay? Stop trying to get something on me."

I held up my hands in a pacifying gesture. "I'm not assigning blame here; I just want the truth. That's all. I want to find Edie. Did you see the girls get in Blount's car?"

Bobbie leaned over and kissed his cheek, murmuring something like, "Afterwards, when she's gone, we can—" That's all I heard. But his face lit up and he looked at me differently now.

"I'm sorry, Miss Matelli. I'm just under a lot of stress. Yes, I did."

"And did you see them drive away?"

Herb looked at Bobbie. She nodded a little. Then

he turned back to me. "Yeah. They drove away."
He was looking a bit uncomfortable.

"Then what did you do?"

That seemed to catch him by surprise. "What did
I do after that?" He let out a noise that sounded like
a cross between a sigh and a rattle.

Bobbie jumped in. "He came back inside, of
course."

I must have looked doubtful because Herb backed
her up quickly. "That's right. I went back in the
house when it looked like he wasn't coming back.
Really, that's all I know."

"Okay," I said, standing up. "Thanks for your
cooperation. I wish you'd go to the police and let
them know that Blount is lying."

Herb's face closed down. "Sorry, I can't do that.
You know why."

It was all I could do to keep from rolling my eyes.

EIGHTEEN

I DIDN'T WANT TO WAKE UP on Sunday morning, but a cheery little ray of sunshine hit me in the eyes. I had to get out of bed to yank the miniblinds the other way, and by that time I was already up so, hell, I figured I may as well make some coffee and toast a bagel. As I was about to split my bagel, I remembered Sunday dinner at Ma's. Couldn't eat anything before then because I had to have room for second and third helpings—Ma expected it.

I'd had a weight problem when I was younger—most of the Matelli girls did. But I could never diet for more than six days at a time when I lived with Ma because by Sunday afternoon, she would be so concerned about whether I was getting enough to eat that she would wear me down to three stuffed artichokes, a Cornish game hen, and a large helping of pasta with no cheese.

These days, I just step up my exercise program if I want to burn calories. Being in the marines took care of my weight problem, and nowadays, one pig-out meal only required three hours of intensive exercise at aikido.

At eleven-thirty, I knocked on Rosa's door. We tumbled into my Corsica and drove to Malden to meet the rest of the family. Ray, my oldest brother, greeted me at Ma's door.

Ray is the achiever. He'd gone into the service

when he was eighteen and served in Vietnam during the last year of the war. After being honorably discharged when he developed a mild case of asthma, he went to the University of Massachusetts on the veteran's bill and became an accountant. Now he headed a small but growing computer company in Connecticut. Despite the fact that he's an accountant, Ray's a funny guy, interested in community theater, and I'm probably closer to him than my other two brothers. He had married right out of school—his wife's name was Helene—and they had two kids, Tommy and Jeff.

He greeted me at the door. "Angie! Haven't seen you for a while." We hugged and patted each other on the back. "When are you going to come down to Connecticut to visit? Helene and the kids want to see you."

"Of course we do," said Helene's low voice from behind Ray. "When are you coming for a visit?" I brushed Helene's cool cheek with my own. She was still as beautiful as the day she married Ray, and that was almost twelve years ago.

"Hey, Ange!" Vinnie greeted me, not getting up from the lounge chair in front of the television, on which the basketball game was loudly playing. Vinnie was my middle brother, and two brothers could not possibly be more different than Vinnie and Ray. Where Ray was slender and darkly handsome, Vinnie had let himself go to fat, a tire around his middle as thick as a boa constrictor, his brassy hair thinning on top, his forehead shiny. "Carla's in the kitchen wit' Ma." He reached for another handful of peanuts in the bowl next to the chair. A sweating beer can sat next to that.

Vinnie had quit high school in his junior year to take a job driving a truck for a local bakery and really hadn't changed his lifestyle in over fifteen years. He'd been married to Carla, his second wife, for three years. His kids, Bobby and Gina, were from his first marriage. Two-year-old Susanna was the product of Vinnie and Carla.

"Where's Albert?" I asked. Ray's four-year-old, Tommy, had his attention, so Vinnie answered.

"You know how it is wit' him, Angie." Vinnie looked troubled for a moment; then his attention wandered back to the game on the tube.

Albert was having marriage problems. He and Sylvia had been on again-off again for over five years. Albert was the youngest of my brothers. We were never sure what he did for a living, and I wasn't sure we wanted to find out. Sometimes he worked as a house painter, other times, he worked as—something. If I was ever called to delve into Albert's life, I'm not sure I'd take the job.

Sophia was coming up the walkway with her kids and Dave in tow. Dave looked a little queasy, as if he wasn't sure this was a good idea. Sophia, on the other hand, glowed.

I'd seen enough of my big sister for the week, so I slipped into the kitchen. Carla was arranging the antipasto on a large platter, and Ma was presiding over a huge bowl of steaming pasta. Ma is a short woman with hair still as black as it was when we were growing up. She claims she's never had to lay a hand on her hair to touch it up, and I believe her—

I know for a fact that Lucrezia down at Hair's the Thing is the one who lays her hands on Ma's hair and keeps it dyed its natural color.

Ma caught sight of me. "Angie! Come help me wit' this. We gotta get it to the table as soon as Sophia and her friend arrive."

"They're here," I said, balancing the serving bowl on one arm like a café waiter.

"Hey, Angie," Carla said as she tucked the antipasto platter into my other arm.

"Hey, yourself," I said with a grin. "Vinnie's put on a little weight."

Carla rolled her eyes. "When basketball season rolls around, he just sits back and watches the games."

As a newlywed, Carla was still looking for advice.

"Yeah, he was like that even when we were growing up." I turned back to Ma. "You make stuffed artichokes?" I loved Ma's stuffed artichokes.

"No, I made Italian beans," Ma said, patting me on the cheek. "The artichokes at the grocery store looked terrible."

I swallowed my disappointment and brought the food out to the table. People were starting to sit down. This would be Dave's trial by fire, I was sure. He caught my eye and I smiled and nodded.

"So this is David." Ma bustled up to Dave, who was seated in the living room next to Vinnie and took his face in her hands, turning his head this way and that to examine it. "Hmmm, no tattoos on the face like that guy with the spiderweb on his forehead."

I stole a sidelong glance at Sophia and saw her

looking down at the floor. Ray, Helene, and Carla looked amused. Vinnie just looked blankly up at Ma.

"What're you doin', Ma?" he said in his plain way. "You're embarrassing the poor guy. Leave him alone. Anyone can see this guy has more class in his little finger than all the guys Sophia's been out with in her entire life." It was the longest speech I'd ever heard coming from Vinnie. There was a short silence while we waited for Ma to respond. Just then, Albert came in the front door.

Albert was Al Pacino-handsome with his classic Roman nose, a narrow chin, and dark, well-defined eyebrows sheltering warm blue eyes. His hair was always razor cut, and he dressed in expensive leather jackets and designer slacks and jeans. The small diamond stud in his left earlobe was new.

With Albert back—and his wife, Sylvia, noticeably absent—the Matelli clan sat down to eat before the meal got cold. We stuffed ourselves on garlic bread, antipasto, stuffed Cornish game hens, pasta, salad, and a number of other things that Ma always made special for us.

When I pushed myself back from the table, I felt about thirty pounds heavier, probably the same feeling expectant mothers get when they're in their third trimester. I looked at my watch and noted that I had about an hour and fifteen minutes before I had to leave to meet Larry and Diane McCarthy in Revere.

"Angie, help Sophia clear the table. Rosa, go with them. The boys don't get much of a chance to get together and talk," Ma ordered, seeming to forget that Sunday dinner was a weekly thing and practically a ritual. "David, let's go in the den and have a little chat." I hadn't really had a chance to talk to Dave since he got here, and I hoped Sophia had prepared him for Ma. She took that family matriarch stuff seriously. Nevertheless, he threw me a look of utter helplessness and I shrugged, giving him what I hoped was a sympathetic look. All I could think about was that cliché about the lamb to the slaughter.

The Matellis did a lot of things that drove me crazy. For instance, we still divided up the men and the women: Women went into the kitchen to cook, wash up afterward, and gossip; men went into the TV room to watch the game and bond. I've always drifted back and forth between the two groups, never completely at home with the domesticity that Matelli women accepted, and never completely accepted by my macho father and brothers. This may be why I ended up in the marines and later as a private investigator.

Many other families, Italian or otherwise, can claim the same sexist setup, but at least some of them are trying to change the way things are done. In our family, Ma likes it that way and doesn't see any need to change things any time soon. Even Ray, whom I considered to be the most enlightened of my three brothers, can get into the whole machismo act.

As I walked into the TV room to gather up stray glasses and plates, Ray called, "Hey, Angie, bring me a beer, will you?" I stopped right in front of him. "You're blocking my view," he complained. Ray tried to crane his neck around my figure. "Hey, hey, I almost missed that sweet shot! Move it, will you?" I continued to glare at him. He finally, reluctantly, tore his eyes away from the Celtics and looked up at me. "What? What'd I say?"

"Ray, stop acting like a moron," I said in a stern tone. "I hope you don't treat Helene like that at home."

The big, dumb Italian look came over his usually intelligent face. "Huh?"

"What is it about coming home? You all revert to Neanderthal behavior?" I mused as I shoved a dirty glass and a stack of plates into his open hands and began thumping my chest with my fists. "Me man, you woman." With that, I sat down on the sofa, narrowly missing Vinnie, who was stretched out on the couch with a can of beer in his hand. "You want a beer so bad, go get it yourself. I'm taking a break."

"Hey!" Vinnie said, sloshing beer on his shirt. "Watch it, Ange."

As Ray got up, muttering about inconsiderate sisters, I stole a glance at Albert. He was looking pensive until he noticed me watching him; then he broke out into a big grin. Damn, he was handsome.

"Don't let 'em get to ya, Angie," he said. When I was growing up, he'd always been the most inaccessible of my brothers. It was the first moment in a long time that I'd felt close to Albert.

An hour before I was supposed to leave to meet with Larry and Diane McCarthy, Sophia pulled me aside and whispered that they—meaning Ma and Dave—had been in that den for what seemed like an hour. She was starting to sweat.

"Hey," I told her, "that's good news. She hasn't let out a screech, and Dave hasn't burst out of the room asking one of us to call nine-one-one yet."

Sophia mulled that over as we gathered up the tablecloth and cloth napkins—Ma liked Sunday dinner to be special. I could hear Rosa playing with the kids down in the rec room, or the "wreck room," as we liked to joke. Carla and Helene were chattering in the kitchen as glasses and dishes clinked and clattered. The brothers let out a shout at a particularly heart-stopping moment of the game.

Just as I was deciding whether to knock on the den door, it opened and a pale but relieved-looking Dave came out, followed by Ma.

She was reaching up to pat him on the shoulder. "Go watch the game with the rest of my boys," she ordered as she marched into the kitchen to oversee the peons.

Dave gave me a wan grin.

"That grueling, huh?" I asked, trying the sympathetic approach.

"She's quite a woman. I can see it in all three of you," he said.

"Did you tell her about your marital status?"

Before he could answer me, we heard Sophia calling him from the kitchen. "Dave! Where are you? I need some help drying the dishes." Ma didn't believe in automatic dishwashers. She already had about twelve able hands during Sunday dinner.

His eyes widened; then he looked toward the kitchen. I was aware that the tension between us had eased up.

"Sounds like the boss is calling."

His eyes were half-closed with that fake confidence that men in love get—the same look teens get when they want to appear cool even though their mother is calling their name. "She can wait a minute."

"Are you free any time tomorrow morning?"

"Depends on what you have in mind," he said with a twinkle in his eye. When he waggled his eyebrows at me, I hit him in the arm.

"Ow!"

"Just because you're dating my sister doesn't mean you have to act like one of my moron brothers," I said. "Besides, this is serious. I need to ask you a couple of questions."

He stopped acting like a goof and agreed that I could come by his office at eight-thirty in the morning. Much too early for me, but I'd manage. After Dave went off to the kitchen, I realized he hadn't told me how the talk with Ma had gone.

Before I could sneak away, Ma came back from the kitchen and summoned me into the den. I hovered by the doorway, ready to make my escape.

"He's a nice man," she said. I waited for the other shoe to drop, but nothing happened. Ma eased into the La-Z-Boy, put her feet up, and rolled her support hose down past her knees. "So, how serious is it between Sophia and David?"

Like I would know. "Well, Sophia seems to be pretty happy with him," I replied, searching for something else to say. While I'd spent time with Dave and time with Sophia, I hadn't spent much quality time with them as a couple. I didn't think the coitus interruptus of a few days ago counted.

A glint from Ma's eyes gave away the intent of this line of questioning. "Do you think there's a chance they'll get married?"

I leaned against the doorway and crossed my arms. "I don't know, Ma. If I could predict the future, I'd be a millionaire."

Ma shifted in the lounger. "Nice boy, that David."

"Yeah, he is," I replied, wondering what time it was getting to be.

"Too bad he's married."

It almost snuck by me. I was about to reply, "Yeah, too bad," when I caught myself. Ma was watching me like a cat ready to pounce on a bug. I remained silent.

"You think I didn't notice?"

"How?" I managed to squeak.

She waved me away. "You didn't notice the ring finger? No ring there now, but he's recently worn one."

That Ma—eyes like a rifle scope, instincts of a lioness. "Look, Ma, I can explain."

"Pah!" Ma heaved herself out of the lounger. "He told me himself. Separated, heading for divorce." She shrugged. "I'm not thrilled, but I want my children to be happy. And this is the happiest I've seen your oldest sister in a long time. Besides," Ma reached out to her right to straighten the magazines on the side table, "he's a lot better than those no-good rebels without a clue she usually hangs out with."

I blinked. This was a side to Ma I never knew about. She seemed to sense my astonishment because she looked straight at me and smiled. "What? You thought I never noticed? Hah! What a mother you'll be someday."

I shuddered at the thought of the patter of little feet and calling some big lug "honeybuns."

"Here's a piece of advice," she continued. "Never expect too much from your children and never criticize their choice of boyfriends or girlfriends or they'll end up marrying the one you hate the most."

I had to admit—it made sense. Ma was smarter than all us kids combined. I decided to make my escape before she told me she knew about Rosa in the pokey. I sneaked a look at my watch. I wanted to be on time to interview the McCarthys.

"Do you need to be somewhere else, Angela Agnes?" Ma asked in that imperious tone that always made me lie to make her happy.

I don't know what I thought would happen if I told the truth, but my involuntary reaction is to say exactly the opposite of what is reality. "No, not really." I waited a beat, collected myself, and did damage control. "Well, actually, I'm supposed to interview this couple who lost their child recently." I launched into the story, focusing on the tragic details.

By the time I was finished, Ma's face was scrunched up like she was going to cry. "Oh, that poor child, those poor parents! How dreadful!" She genuflected and looked up at the ceiling, as if God were looking right down at us. "We've never had a tragedy like that in our family and I hope we never will." I was positive the big guy was listening to her and taking notes, the way she spoke so intimately to him.

I felt my stomach tighten, realizing that talking about it had helped me understand the consequences much better. I was eager to get on with the investigation, eager to look at it from a new angle.

Ma came over and gave me a hug. I could smell the garlic and tomato sauce on her. She wore it like a fine perfume. Then she drew back and patted my cheek, a smile on her face and a tear in her eye. "You're a good girl, Angela Matelli."

"You're a pretty good ma, Ma," I replied.

I got a wet kiss on my cheek; then Ma walked me to the door. "You find that other little girl alive, okay?" she told me. "And get the son of a bitch who did it."

I waved from the sidewalk and got in my Corsica, heading for Revere and the McCarthys.

NINETEEN

LARRY AND DIANE MCCARTHY lived in a nice area of Revere, near Point of Pines. Situated on a two-acre lot, the McCarthy house was a sprawling three-story Victorian that was in the process of being restored. Half the house was scraped down to the bare wood and the other half had been painted a light gray. The fishscale and herringbone patterns under the eaves had been painted white with maroon trim. It wasn't a Queen Anne Victorian with all the lacy gingerbread trim, but was a nice example of the solid Victorian that was more popular with upper-middle-class families of that era.

Me? I preferred the redbrick three-story apartment building I lived in that overlooked Boston Bay. Still, I was curious to see the inside. I'd always had an interest in New England architecture.

Larry McCarthy was a tall man with friendly features partially obscured by a beard and glasses. "You must be Ms. Matelli," he said, shaking my hand as I stepped inside the foyer. The interior of the house was as warm as the man I'd just met, although I got the impression the renovation had come to a standstill.

"We just moved to Massachusetts in August and were in the middle of painting the outside and redecorating the inside," he explained quietly. "But when Rachel disappeared…" There was no need to say more. I understood that the house had been left the way it was, both inside and out, when Rachel was murdered.

McCarthy led me into the den, a cozy front room about the size of my living room and kitchen combined. A tall, striking woman with bobbed copper hair sat on an overstuffed velvet sofa. When I came in, she stood up and extended her hand. From her poise and her model-thin good looks, I guessed that she might have been a model or an actress at one time. I had read someplace that when someone died in a household during the Victorian era, families draped the windows, pictures, and mirrors in black cloth. Although there wasn't a black cloth in sight, I couldn't help but notice the overwhelming sadness that permeated the place.

After I declined their offer of a drink, the McCarthys sat together on the sofa, presenting a united front. I thought this was unusual and rather touching. When a child dies of unnatural causes, it often causes a rift between the parents. "Should have's" and "If I'd only's" begin to enter the picture—"You should have let her eat that last piece of cake" and "If only I'd said no when she told me she wanted to go over to Sarah's house for the night." Guilt and blame become constants in the marriage and eventually, statistically, parents of murdered children ended up divorced, each living with their own particular brand of hell.

Diane began warily. "Larry told me that you wanted to talk to us about Rachel. I hope you're not here to try to get something from us."

Larry intercepted whatever else she was going to

say. "What Diane is trying to say is that we've been approached by everyone from psychics to ambulance-chasers, everyone wanting to play on our grief."

"Usually wanting money for information they may have or may be able to get," Diane finished drily.

"That's not my intention," I began. "I'm here trying to find a link between Rachel's death and Edie's disappearance."

Worry clouded their expressions. "I didn't know Edie was missing," Larry said.

"She disappeared around the same time Rachel did," I explained.

Diane looked mystified. "Is there a missing persons report on her as well?"

"Well, you see, her mother thought that Edie had gone back to her father in California."

Diane looked dubious. "Didn't she call to check on her fourteen-year-old daughter?"

I shrugged. What could I say? The McCarthys exchanged glances, as if they knew it was a stupid question.

"The thing is, I've found a connection." I briefly explained about my eyewitness.

Larry's hands were clenched into fists. "Can't we make him tell the truth to the police?"

I shrugged in a helpless manner. "He can deny everything and claim that I'm lying. Not everyone is an upstanding citizen."

"Who is the guy this witness claimed to see?" Larry asked.

I hadn't mentioned Blount's name. "I can't reveal

that, but I will be questioning him further. And I'll tell the police what the witness told me as well. There's just not much they can do about it if this guy doesn't come forward.''

''It's just not fair,'' Diane said softly. Her mouth trembled and she took a deep breath.

I changed the subject. ''Can you tell me a little bit about Rachel and Edie's friendship?''

Diane began to talk about Edie and Rachel. ''We hadn't known Edie for long, but since the girls had both moved here at the beginning of the school year, they became fast friends at school. You know how kids who grow up in the same area all their lives have their little cliques. Edie and Rachel were the outsiders.''

''Did Edie seem unhappy at all?''

''Of course,'' Larry said. ''She talked about her father all the time. Talked about wanting to go back to him. We offered to help her, but she would suddenly turn reluctant.''

''She confided in Rachel, though,'' Diane added.

''Edie must have confided a lot in Rachel,'' I said. ''Did Rachel seem disturbed or did she act differently just before she disappeared?''

Both McCarthys lowered their eyes as if the thought of what happened next was too painful to think about. And I'm sure it was. ''Yes,'' Diane replied in a whisper. ''She used to tell us all the time about Edie and her problems. But the last few days, God forgive me for not noticing until it was too late, she stopped talking about Edie altogether.''

I hated to bring up the next part of my interview, but it had to be done. And sometimes it helped the grieving parents to talk about it. I leaned forward. "Tell me about Rachel."

A melancholy look stole over Larry's face. Diane glanced away. Unlike her husband, she struck me as someone who didn't like to display her emotions to a stranger.

After a few moments of silence, Larry was the first to speak. "She was turning into such a beautiful girl."

Diane stood up and walked to the other side of the room, where she took a photograph in a beaten silver frame off of a table. She handed it to me. It was one of those studio pictures with soft lighting and a muted background. The slender, poised girl in the picture had long, straight, strawberry blonde hair and large brown eyes. She was one of those girls I had always envied in junior high. Rachel had perfect dimples when she smiled, whereas my dimples had come from being chubby. Somewhere between adolescence and adulthood, I lost the weight, and the dimples went with them. Rachel's dimples would have stayed with her forever.

"She's lovely," I said, meaning it. I handed the photograph back to Diane, who avoided my attempt at direct eye contact.

"She was about three weeks away from turning fourteen. We were planning a party for her," Larry said, his voice breaking slightly. He looked down at his large hands and blinked several times. "The day she… left, she had stayed after at school. She was part of the debate team."

"Was Edie part of the debate team as well?"

Diane answered from across the room as she returned the framed photograph to its rightful place. "No, she wasn't."

"That's why no one thought to ask about her," I said more to myself than to them. I brought my attention back to them. "What time was Rachel supposed to be home?"

"About four o'clock," Larry said.

"It was Friday afternoon," Diane elaborated, "and on Fridays, because the debate group met from two-thirty to three-thirty, Edie and Rachel didn't usually get together."

"What about Edie's mom?" I asked.

The McCarthys exchanged another glance, as if they were reluctant to talk badly about someone else, but couldn't think of anything good to say, either.

"What about her?" Larry asked in a wary tone.

"I assume you met her once or twice. What were your impressions of her?"

Diane gave a loud sigh, sat up a little straighter, and placed her hands on her knees as if bracing herself for an unpleasant subject. "At one time, we thought we might call the Department of Children's Services about Em and the way she treated Edie. It was a disgrace."

Larry put his hand on her arm. "But we just let it be known that it was all right with us if Edie stayed overnight frequently. We figured at least that way she'd have some stability."

"Staying out all night, not leaving food in the house for her little girl," Diane began the angry litany, "and bringing home those awful men." She crossed her arms and trembled as if she were cold, but I didn't think it was from the temperature.

I felt a little cold as well.

I turned the interview back to Rachel. Call it curiosity. "Can you tell me what sort of leads the police had in Rachel's death?" Using the words "death" and "Rachel" in the same sentence sounded harsher than I'd intended, but the McCarthys didn't seem to notice. No doubt over the past week, they'd had plenty of experience getting used to those two words in the same sentence.

They looked at each other, apparently reluctant to get into details. Couldn't blame them. But I prodded them. "When I first started looking for Edie, Rachel's name came up and as I've said before, there may be a connection since they both disappeared about the same time and they were good friends."

That seemed to satisfy Diane. "Well, the police interviewed our housekeeper, but she only comes in twice a month. Still, she was here the day before Rachel was—" She seemed at a loss about how to end. I didn't help her. I got the picture.

Larry jumped in. "All the grandparents were interviewed, and my sister, who lives nearby."

"Were there any other friends, any school connections?"

"I think the police interviewed everyone on the debating team who was present at the last meeting that Friday."

They gave me a list of names from the debate team. It would help if MacMillan didn't feel inclined to give me the information they'd already gathered.

I ended the interview with the usual "If you think of anything else of significance, here's my card," when the McCarthys gave each other another eloquent look. Larry cleared his throat.

"Uh, Ms. Matelli, we talked about this before you got here, and Diane agrees with me." He stood up and went over to a walnut desk with an Oriental-Victorian look to it and picked up something from the surface. Crossing the room, he offered a plain white envelope to me.

"It's a retainer," he explained. "That's what you need, right?"

I opened my mouth to say something, but then I looked up into his trusting brown eyes. I felt like a creep.

"Uh, Mr. and Mrs. McCarthy," I said, "I didn't come here to be hired by you...."

Diane McCarthy stood up and walked over to stand next to her husband. "We did a little checking and were assured by the police that you were a good investigator. I hope you don't mind, but we'd like you to look into Rachel's murder."

"We know the police are doing everything they can, but it can't hurt to have a private investigator on the case," Larry said. He shook the envelope at me. I gingerly took it and laid it aside on an end table.

"I already have a client—" I began. Actually, technically, I was working for Ev since Detective Holmes had finished his initial investigation.

But I hadn't talked to Detective MacMillan yet about his investigation on Edie. Presumably he had reopened Rachel's case, but both MacMillan and Holmes had made it clear that I could investigate if

I brought them any evidence I found regarding Rachel's murder.

Larry McCarthy ducked his head and ran a hand across the back of his neck. Diane blinked several times and looked away.

"We were hoping you could act as a liaison between us and the police," she said, reaching down to pick up a different framed picture on the end table near me. She held it out and I looked at it. This was a more carefree Rachel, a Rachel who hadn't been carefully posed and lighted from the right angles. The grinning young girl who looked back at me was definitely on vacation, somewhere on a New England boardwalk with the gray-blue Atlantic behind her. She wore peach shorts and a T-shirt with a picture of a lobster in a trap and the words Trapped in Maine on it. Her teeth were a little crooked, and a white billed cap perched on reddish blond braids.

"This picture was taken in Bar Harbor last year," Larry said. "It just doesn't seem fair that she should die like that and the murderer gets away scot-free."

"Would it really compromise you to be working two cases that might have a connection?" Diane asked.

I know they didn't intend to intimidate me, but sitting there with two grief-stricken parents looming over me made me feel at a disadvantage. I stood. Larry retrieved the envelope from the end table and extended it toward me.

I took it.

TWENTY

WHEN I GOT BACK to my apartment, Holmes had already dropped off a copy of the polygraph questions. They were pretty much what I would have asked both Blount and Cooper, with one exception.

I checked my answering machine. Mark had called to let me know that Edie wasn't in the runaway network here in Boston. He said that he'd keep checking and had put in a call to a national runaway network. I called Mark back to thank him.

There was also another message from Joe Blount, politely asking if I'd update him on my progress in finding Edie. *In your dreams, pal,* I thought. I got paid for that sort of thing. If Earlene wasn't getting a report, he certainly wasn't getting one.

I spent the rest of Sunday evening in my apartment drawing doodles around the one question that hadn't made it onto the polygraph test questions: Did you see Rachel McCarthy and Edie Morrow again *after* you dropped them off at the Revere beachfront seawall?

Then I made up a list of what I knew about the case and what I needed to know. Blount had lied about where he had met Edie and Rachel, but I couldn't understand how he had passed the lie detector test. While the test isn't foolproof, a lie as big as this usually doesn't go undetected.

Rachel had been molested before she was killed.

I would have to talk to Blount's ex-wife, Sally, and see what her thoughts were on Blount's behavior around children. He didn't seem to have a record of molestation, but my gut feeling was that there was more to the divorce than his drunken behavior.

I debated about whether to contact MacMillan and Holmes with what I'd discovered. I knew I shouldn't hold out information on a suspect, but my one witness was reluctant to come forward and, if questioned, would just deny everything. So I decided to wait and find out what I could from Sally Blount. At least I'd have some ammunition to hand MacMillan and Holmes.

On Monday morning, I went into my office before eight, intending to catch up on some filing. Another message from Joe Blount. The man was a little too eager—suspicious behavior to me. Even Edie's mother hadn't bugged me that much. For that matter, Ev hadn't, either.

I figured that if Sally Blount had the children during the school week, she would be up early to get her children off to school. I'd found her listed in the Revere phone directory easily. She answered when I'd called. After I explained why I wanted to talk to her, there was a short silence on her end of the phone.

"Mrs. Blount? Are you still there?"

"Yes, I'm thinking."

I could see this was going to be a sales job. "Look, I'm sorry if this is too painful for you to want to talk about, but a young girl is dead and another girl has been missing for over a week. Her mother is really getting worried." Instinct told me to mention

Edie's mother, and not her father, when trying to convince Blount's ex to talk to me. I wasn't sure if a father's concern would push this woman to the point where she would talk about her marriage to Joe Blount.

She agreed to see me in the late morning. "I have a few errands to run; then I'll be here an hour or two before the kids get home for lunch." She gave me directions to her house, and we hung up. I looked at my watch and got ready to meet Dave at his office.

I WAS A LITTLE EARLY when I stepped into the outer lobby of Dave's office. Although the reception window was still dark, the door was ajar to the inner sanctum—Dave's office—and he was squatting to pull a giant medical text from the bottom shelf of his ceiling-to-floor bookcase.

He looked up when I walked in. "Angie. Good to see you." He stood up and went around to sit at his desk, the textbook making a heavy thumping sound on the desk's surface. I caught a look at the title: *The Child in All of Us.*

"I'd think with an imposing volume like that, the title would be something more scholarly and boring," I said.

Dave gave me a blank look, then looked down at the book. His face cleared. "Yeah, I know what you mean. But even us scholarly types are suckers for catchy titles."

I sat down in a nice comfortable chair, the kind that makes you want to start telling your life story to the guy behind the desk. "So you never did tell me about your talk with Ma. How did it go?"

His expression was inscrutable. "How do you think it went? We talked about my work; then we talked about ungrateful children and how to deal with them."

Dave may be a child psychologist, but Ma was a homegrown psychologist.

I chuckled. "And she asked you about the tan line on your ring finger."

His face went red, but he smiled, then laughed along with me and nodded. "Yeah, it did come up. We talked and she seemed to take to me."

"Ma said you were a nice boy." I started giggling. I don't giggle well, and it only happens when something strikes me as absurd. If I try to control it, the giggle gets worse. When we stopped long enough to take a couple of deep breaths, Dave put on his glasses, the ones with the thin red plastic rims, and leaned back in his chair. "So tell me what you're here for, Angie. I know it wasn't just to talk over what your mother had to say about me."

I explained the case, glossing over stuff that wasn't applicable and finally getting to Joe Blount.

He absently tapped his upper lip with a pencil he'd picked up. "You want me to give you a psychological profile of a child molester?"

"If there's such a thing," I said, suspecting I was asking for the impossible.

Dave frowned in thought. "Well, there's no one type of child molester, but they do have a few things in common. First, they have a personality disorder."

"What's a personality disorder?" I asked.

He thought about that one. "It's not a disease or anything like that, it's just a part of their personality that never developed, or that developed in a lopsided way. A guy who's an asshole all the time, who constantly picks fights, or who enjoys screwing people over, that's a personality disorder.''

"Hell, I knew a lot of guys with personality disorders in the military,'' I cracked.

"Molesters like to hang around children, and like to play like children.'' He could see he was losing me, so he got up and paced around, as if that was going to help. "What I mean by playing *like* children is that they pout and fight like a child when they're playing with others.''

None of this was of any help to me. But I knew that both Herb Cooper and Joe Blount drank. "What about alcohol? Can that play a part, maybe set loose some subliminal molester in a man who's got a tight rein on his thoughts and feelings when he's sober?''

Dave nodded slowly. "That's a possibility. Alcohol releases inhibitions, fantasies, or urges.''

"What about drinking to excess, to the point of blacking out and sexually abusing a child?''

"Many of us believe that alcohol is just an excuse for sexual abuse. There are several schools of thought on sexual abuse and molesters, but one thing is clearly defined, and that's the definition of a pedophile.''

"What's that?''

He picked up a large volume and read from it. "'A pedophile is a subject or person who forces sexual activity with children.''' He looked over the rims of his glasses at me. "It says here that to be labeled a pedophile, he or she must sexually abuse children for a total of six months. Personally, I think that definition sucks donkeys.''

''So in other words,'' I said in a dry tone, ''I could sexually abuse a kid for a total of five months, three weeks, and six days and not be a pedophile?''

Dave sat back down behind his desk, clasped his hands, and leaned forward. ''Look, Angie, I have to tell you that psychology is an inexact science. Your perp might be a guy who follows all the rules when he's sober, but can't tell the difference between a teenage girl and a grown woman when he's had too many drinks. And it's very possible that he could be doing all this during a blackout.''

I was starting to get an idea. ''Okay, I get it.''

Dave smiled indulgently and looked at his watch. ''Anything else, Angie?''

I snuck a look at mine as well and realized I had about five minutes left. ''So what I want to know is—and this may not be totally in your field, but give me as good an answer as possible—can a guy who's killed someone during a blackout pass a polygraph test?''

Dave fingered his clean-shaven chin. ''Hmmm. Interesting question. Normally, I'd have to refer you to someone else, but a few weeks ago, I attended a seminar on polygraphs.''I raised my eyebrows. The man was a veritable fountain of knowledge. He gave me a mock-stern look. ''Well, I was interested in the subject, and it can relate indirectly to my field.''

''Are there ways to beat it?'' Something nagged at the back of my mind, something that fit in with this line of questioning, but I couldn't put my finger on it.

"Well, to answer your first question, yes. There have been some cases of alcoholics who killed someone during a blackout and couldn't recall the act. And I would think that if that were the case, it wouldn't be too hard to pass the test." Dave stood up and walked over to his library. He pulled out a book and thumbed through it until he came to a page. "As for how you beat it, there are several ways. You can take certain drugs that deaden your physical response, keeping your heartbeat, pulse, and other polygraph factors within a certain range. Another way is to train yourself to not react. If you know what questions are coming—and usually with polygraphs, you are shown the questions beforehand—you won't respond as drastically if you prepare yourself. Then there's always the tack in the shoe method."

Something in my mind clicked. I'd heard about it once before. Someone who wants to beat a lie detector can place a tack in their shoe and press down on it whenever he or she is asked a control question. Although the entire test response has been heightened, it still falls within the normal range of tests: neither completely guilty, nor totally innocent.

"Well, that was helpful," I replied pensively.

Dave shook his head a little and said, "I know this all sounds vague, but human behavior is unpredictable."

I sighed and stood up. "Well, I thought it might give me some insight into Joe Blount and Herb Cooper."

"You mean, you wanted an easy answer."

I gave him a sheepish look. "Yeah, I guess so. You zeroed in on my behavior pretty closely."

He laughed. "That was easy. I listened to you, I watched your body language, and I heard what was going on behind the words." He showed me to the door. "I hope you get your man, Angie, and find the girl. Let me know if I can be of any help. Maybe if you ask the right questions of Blount's ex-wife, you might find your answers. By the way, will you be coming back to class?"

We hadn't talked about it, but it had been almost a week since I'd been to my last class. I felt comfortable with him now, and gave him a warm look. "Yeah. I'll be at the dojo this Wednesday."

"Good. We miss you." From the way he looked at me, I could tell it was over—the embarrassment, the discomfort, all of it unspoken.

"Thanks. I missed you guys, too." I paused at the door. "Hey, Dave?" He looked up from a chart. "I love it when you play psychologist." I think the chart hit the door as I walked out.

His patient was in the waiting room, her sullen look fitting right in with the torn jeans, tight top, and too much makeup—a Bobbie Matthews in the making. I smiled at her, and was rewarded with a glare, hugging herself as if she might fall apart if she let go. Maybe I reminded her of her mother. That was a scary thought.

I went straight to my appointment with Sally Blount. She lived in a detached town house, one of the attempts made to give Revere a new, upscale look. It didn't take. Surrounding the town house were small, older clapboard houses, some that had been boarded up. Graffiti artists had made their own attempt to brighten up the neighborhood by scrawling misspelled messages full of "fucks" and "screws" and "shits" and "cocksuckers"—the only words that were spelled correctly.

Sally met me at the door with a small boy underfoot. He was about four years old, a sunny blond with a dimpled smile and blue eyes. It was hard to believe that Sally Blount wasn't his grandmother. She clearly had led a hard life. Lines etched her forehead, deep grooves ran from nose to mouth, and her body seemed to have sagged and settled at her hips. Still, when she smiled at me, I could see that she had once been a very pretty woman.

"You must be Angela Matelli," she said, letting me into her house. I was surprised at how clean and neat everything was. Here was a woman who apparently spent all her time and energy on keeping an orderly house. The furniture was older, but in good condition. The house smelled of Lysol and potpourri, and the walls were a warm, pale yellow. I caught a glimpse of the kitchen, which seemed to suffer from the current country goose fever. A blue band dotted with white geese marched around the walls, and the refrigerator was covered with goose magnets. It wasn't my taste, but it was homey.

"You have a lovely home," I said as I sat on the calico sofa.

She beamed. "Thank you. Would you like some coffee? I just made a fresh pot."

She brought out two mugs, and I began by recounting the case. She nodded in the right places and frowned when appropriate. When I started to tell her about her ex-husband and where he fit in, it was hard to tell what her reaction was. It didn't change—she kept nodding and tsk-tsking in the right places, but I didn't feel as if I was getting a true reaction. I finally came to the end and took a sip of coffee, hoping to hear from her. She didn't disappoint me.

"Miss Matelli," she began, "I spent the last few hours trying to decide what to tell you, how much I wanted to tell you." She averted her eyes. The boy, whose name I had learned was Jason, was quietly playing nearby with a Lego set. He started to chew on a small piece. "Jason, take that out of your mouth right now or we put the Legos away."

Jason reluctantly pulled it out of his mouth and tossed it on the rug.

She turned back to me, an apologetic smile on her face. "I'm sitting for his mother, who lives next door."

"It must have been a hard decision to make," I replied. "He is the father of your children, and putting him through the legal system would be heartbreaking for them."

She held up her hand. "You're right. That was part of it. But I also realize that Joe needs help, and by letting him get away with something"—she paused, then quickly added—"if he did this, it wouldn't be in anyone's best interest."

I was betting that she had talked to a counselor after our phone call. A lot of what she was saying to me sounded like it was secondhand, word for word. But I didn't stop her. Sally closed her eyes and took a deep breath. "Okay. I'm committed. Go ahead and ask your questions. I'll answer them as honestly as I can.''

"Mrs. Blount, why did you divorce your husband?''

It took her a moment to answer, as if she had to formulate it in her mind first. "I tell everyone that it was his drinking that led to the divorce, and that's partly true. But in the last few months of our marriage, I knew that something was wrong. My daughter, Julie, began to withdraw. I realized she was moody on the days after Joe came home from a drinking binge. It had begun to happen more and more frequently.'' Sally stopped and sipped her coffee. "One night, I woke up when I heard Julie cry out from her room. I went down the hall to investigate, and when I opened her door—'' She covered her mouth with her hand and closed her eyes as if to stop the tears from coming. "This is very difficult to talk about, Miss Matelli. Where was I? I saw my husband—ex-husband—on top of Julie and she was crying. I felt as if I'd stood there for hours, but it must have been only half a minute.''

"What did you do then?'' I asked.

"Please understand, Joe was never a violent drunk. He never hit me, or our children. In a lot of ways, he's a good father. But when he drinks, well—'' She gestured to finish the sentence, then continued. "I rushed into the room and pulled him off of her, screaming at him and covering Julie's body with my own. He tried to pull me off a few times, then gave up and staggered into our bedroom.'' She got up with her coffee cup and went into the kitchen for a refill, raising her voice to finish her story. "Anyway, in the morning, I confronted him, but he swore he didn't know what I was talking about. That's when I filed charges of statutory rape and later for divorce."

"But there's no record of the charges," I said, knowing what Sally was going to tell me next.

She came back in and sat down with a big sigh. "I know it was probably the wrong decision, but Julie and I talked about it and she wanted to drop the charges against her daddy. Since I was already going through with the divorce, Julie decided she would be all right if she only saw her dad in supervised situations and never spent the night at his place. I went along with it, but there are times I've regretted my decision."

"Julie is seeing a counselor, I take it."

Sally nodded. "We all are—the boys, Julie, me. Joe refuses to go. He says it's our problem and he still won't acknowledge what happened that night. He doesn't believe Julie, and he doesn't believe me."

"It took a lot of courage to do what you and Julie did," I said. I admired her. Here was a woman who hadn't been immobilized by indecision. She just went ahead and did what she thought was right. It was refreshing to hear a story like hers, but it was also frustrating that Joe Blount's police record didn't show the charges.

"Don't get me wrong, Miss Matelli," Sally said. "I don't think Joe is a raving child molester like so many examples we've seen in articles and on talk shows."

I recalled my discussion with Dave this morning and tried to understand. In my book, Blount was slime, but obviously this woman had loved him at one time.

"You have to understand, my therapist has talked to me about this," she said. "She says that Joe's alcoholism causes him to black out, but he continues to act fairly normal. Yet if you tell him things he did the night before, he doesn't remember. When he drinks, he loses his inhibitions and his ability to tell right from wrong. When he molested Julie, he wasn't thinking of her age or the fact that she was his daughter. She was just available. Joe swears it only happened the one time. The time I caught him in her room."

Once would be enough for me. "So what you're saying is that your ex wasn't necessarily interested in teenage girls. But when he drinks, he just can't tell the difference between an underage girl and a consenting adult woman." I felt as if I were parroting what Dave had told me earlier.

She seemed to consider what I'd said, then nodded. "That's essentially it." She shrugged. "I don't know if this will be of help to you."

"Do you think your ex-husband is capable of killing someone when he's been drinking?"

She shook her head. "Not on purpose. When I was protecting Julie that night, he did get a little rough, but not homicidal."

"What exactly did he do that night when you were keeping him from Julie?" I asked.

She looked down. "First he tried to pull me off her, saying that it wasn't how it looked. Then he punched me a couple of times, but they were half-hearted punches. Then he went for my throat, but

Julie screamed and my oldest boy, Ralph, came in and pulled him off of us.''

We talked a bit longer before I thanked her and started to leave. Sally stopped me at the door. ''Just for the record, I hope he didn't do this,'' she said. ''Because if he did, I don't know what it's going to do to our children. They've been through enough.''

''So have the parents of the girls who are dead and missing,'' I pointed out.

She slumped against the door and gave me a weak smile. ''I know. I'm just venting. My counselor says it's good to vent.''

As I turned to leave, I could hear her voice through the door. ''Jason, leave that outlet alone or I won't let you watch cartoons later.''

TWENTY-ONE

I GOT HOME and took a hot shower. I'd wanted to take a nice long bath, but I was afraid I'd fall asleep in the tub and wake up as wrinkled as a golden raisin. As I slipped between my sheets, I waited for the sandman to come along, but I guess he was on a break. After an hour of tossing and turning and staring at the clock, I got up and made some coffee.

I pulled out my paper placemat from Shari's Diner with all my notes on it and reviewed it. I ticked off most of the items—Blount had lied, but had just confessed the truth.

I was very interested in getting Rachel's murderer, but I was more interested in finding Edie. There were three possibilities—Edie had either run away, was being held captive, or she was dead.

Only a few people had seen Edie on a regular basis over the past few months. I looked at the placemat again—who else had lied?

Herb Cooper had his secret condo. It wasn't really a lie, but a lie by omission. What was wrong with that picture? He had a condo, yet he schtupped Bobbie at her house in front of her kids. What's the deal?

I called Bobbie's place of work and she answered. When I identified myself, she sounded less than pleased to hear from me.

"Don't tell me," she said in what I took to be a

sarcastic tone, "more questions. And I'm not waking Herb up."

"Just a couple of questions, Bobbie."

"Shoot."

"Herb has a condo, doesn't he?"

She was silent for a moment. "Yes, he did, but he couldn't afford to keep it. It's up for sale. We still go there occasionally."

"But he hasn't sold it yet, right?"

"Not that I know of." Her voice was thoughtful. "Come to think of it, we haven't gone there in the last week or two."

I changed directions. "Bobbie, how well did Herb know Edie?"

She opened up a bit. "They talked quite a bit. She was interested in his print shop, and he told her that when she got a little older, he'd hire her to help him around the shop—you know, sort of an apprentice. I think she'd been to his shop several times."

That was interesting. Herb had told me that he hardly knew her to talk to her. "Would you say he was sort of a substitute father for her?"

"Yeah, sure. Look, I gotta get back to work. The male strippers from down the street just walked in."

"One more question, Bobbie. Do you have the address of the condo?"

She gave it to me and I called the police station and left a message for MacMillan. I thought about calling Ev as well, but if I was wrong, I didn't want to look like a complete idiot.

Armed with the address, I drove out to Herb Cooper's condo in Nahant, a little town on a finger of land that stuck out from northern Massachusetts between Saugus and Lynn. It was a nice vacation spot, close to Boston, yet far enough away to relax. And it wasn't part of the overcrowded, overpopular Cape Cod, a Massachusetts native's idea of a vacation in hell during the summer. I was willing to bet that if the dreaded Marian Cooper found out about Herb's little lovenest, he might not live to close on the sale of the condo.

The crickets were chirruping, the frogs were croaking, and all the other night noises of nature were adding to the din when I arrived at the Cooper condo. It was situated near a wooded area about three blocks from the ocean—of course, anywhere you lived in Nahant, you'd be near Massachusetts Bay. There were no lights on inside the condominium units; in fact, there were no cars in the lot. These were vacation units and it was October. I was glad I'd left a working flashlight in my glove compartment.

I shined my light on the two doors that faced the lot, looking for unit number three, and when I didn't see it, I decided it must be around back, facing the woods. As I walked around the building, I swore I heard footsteps behind me, but when I stopped and listened, I heard nothing. I quickened my pace, hoping I'd find that Edie was staying here.

I had to climb a set of outside stairs to find the third unit. My knock echoed, and I strained to hear something in the condo, something that might tell me Edie was there. I was starting to think that my hunch was wrong when I heard a sound from inside. It could have been a mouse, but I wasn't going away without checking the inside of that condo unit.

I ran through some possibilities: If Herb had killed Rachel, why take Edie captive and keep her alive? It made no sense. In for one murder, in for a dozen, was usually how a killer thought.

My instinct told me that Herb Cooper was no killer. If he was guilty of anything, it was poor judgment—aiding a minor in running away, giving her a place to hide out, not counseling her to go to the police. Herb didn't strike me as swift.

I turned the knob, but the door was locked. Of course. I shined my flashlight through the side window. It was an open living room/kitchen arrangement. I could see a fake fireplace to one side and signs of life on the kitchen counter—fast food wrappers and cups.

There was no one around; this part of Nahant was practically a ghost town this late in the fall. I called out. "Edie? Can you hear me? My name is Angela Matelli," I said in a loud voice that seemed to echo in this quiet area. "Your father hired me to find you. He's very worried about you—"

There was the click of a latch being drawn back; then the safety chain was removed. Finally, the door was open a crack and the eye of a tall, slender girl who resembled the Edie I once knew, the Edie of Ev's photo, stared out at me. At first her sliver of an expression looked relieved; then it turned to curiosity.

"Edie? It's okay," I said. "I'm here to take you back to your father."

She looked at me, puzzled. "Do I know you from somewhere?" She had stepped back enough to allow me to step inside, but not enough to close the door.

I took out my business card and handed it to her. She studied it.

"You may remember me from years ago. I was in the corps with your dad."

Her face lit up and she nodded. "Yeah, Matelli. He used to talk about the stuff you two did back then." She wrinkled her nose. "I was just a little kid." Her pleasant expression turned to horror just about the time I heard the footsteps behind me. But I didn't have a chance to turn around. Someone hit me across the back of the head, took me by the shoulders, and dragged me outside. I was on the edge of the steps, trying to recover my balance, teetering and flailing my arms as I sailed out, helped by a hand between my shoulder blades.

I heard Edie cry "Angela!" just before I began my slow tumble down the stairs.

"Get away from me! Leave me alone!" Edie screamed, and there was a scuffling sound, then a thud and a crash.

I landed roughly at the bottom of the stairs, jarring my spine. But it shook me up enough to get me motivated. Why hadn't I brought my gun? I'd left it in the desk drawer back in my office again.

Everything was spinning so fast. I squeezed my eyes closed to stop the dizziness. When I opened them, I saw the railing that led up to the unit and I reached out for it. It seemed to take me forever to stand up and get my bearings. I wasn't hearing any noise coming from the condo, but the door was open. I looked around for my flashlight and found it about five feet away from me. I picked it up and tried to turn it on, but it wouldn't work. I hefted it. The metal casing could still be a makeshift weapon, I reasoned, if I needed it. Unless there was another way out, I figured the attacker and Edie were still in the condo. I may have been disoriented from my tumble down the stairs, but I knew they couldn't have gotten past me.

I climbed the stairs, gaining more of my equilibrium back with each step. I worried about Edie. From the glimpse I'd gotten of her, she had started to trust me before the killer found her. And now, if she was still alive and had gotten away from my attacker, she would probably never trust me again. Herb Cooper was familiar with the area, but if Joe Blount was the killer, had I led him straight to her? I was betting on Blount, but I wasn't sure how he had found this place, unless he'd had me under surveillance all day.

The door was open and I stepped inside. The condo seemed to be empty on my first tour. A pair of jeans, a couple of T-shirts and flannel shirts, and a Star Wars sleeping bag lay on the empty floor of what would probably be the living room. Edie also had a Walkman next to her sleeping bag, and there were several tapes scattered around the floor. I squatted and examined the tapes by the dim moonlight— mostly Seattle grunge rock bands like Pearl Jam and Nirvana.

I was wasting time, so I moved quickly into the kitchen. A beat-up aluminum pot sat on the stove, crusted over with something that looked like canned chili. I looked around the kitchen for a better weapon than the flashlight, but couldn't even come up with a butter knife.

In the bathroom, there was nothing more than a

wet towel hanging on a hook on the back of the door. The bathtub had a ring around it. The bedroom was empty except for a couple of coat hangers in the closet.

Back in the living room, I looked for another way out. Could they have gotten past me? I was starting to doubt my own sanity. But I was sure I would have noticed a man dragging a screaming kid down the stairs. That's when I noticed the hallway at the other end of the living room. There was an open front door that led to a stairway. I hadn't noticed it when I was looking out front because it was concealed from the outside. Maybe if it were daytime, I would have noticed it.

I took it slow, wielding the flashlight like a miniature bat, making sure the killer wasn't waiting for me around a corner. Then I clambered down the stairs and stumbled out the front entrance. I spied a tall, dark figure having trouble carrying a smaller figure—Edie—as he made his way toward the street to a car parked down the road. I did the only thing I could.

"Stop!" I yelled as I broke into an easy run. "Get away from her, you pervert!" I was hoping there might be someone taking a late vacation in the neighborhood, but I didn't see any lights come on. But I faked it, pretending there was a neighbor out on her front porch without the lights on. "Hey, lady! Call the police!" I shouted to no one. "There's a man trying to abduct a little girl."

The figure stopped and cursed, then tossed the figure he had been carrying onto the grass. He cut to his right and ran toward the woods. I hesitated between checking on Edie to see if she was all right and catching the bastard. Edie won out—she was my priority.

When I got to her, I bent over her and laid my fingers on the side of her neck. She still had a pulse, but her eyelids fluttered. She opened her eyes and looked up at me. Then she gave me a sick smile.

"Are you okay?" I asked.

"Yes," she breathed. "But I don't feel good."

I wasn't feeling all that well myself, but I didn't want to let on. I smiled back at her. "Let's get you into my car and we'll get out of here." I helped her up—she was light—and wrapped one of her arms around my neck and my arm around her waist. I noticed that I wasn't much taller than she was. We made our way to my Corsica, and I put her gently on the passenger seat, then closed the door. I got in the driver's side and cranked the ignition.

"So, you're not a marine anymore," Edie said in a faint tone.

I smiled. "Once a marine, always a marine," I replied, using the motto that we marines felt deeply. I was still feeling a little faint from the attack, which showed in the wobbly way I drove down the street. I was relieved that Nahant was seemingly deserted. "I live in Boston now and have a private investigator's license." Not that she didn't know that already from my business card, but it's a great conversation starter when you've just gotten away from a killer. I wanted to calm Edie down before I started asking questions.

"Cool." She turned her head to stare out the passenger-side window. "How's my dad?"

"He's fine," I replied. I stopped at a stop sign, then accelerated beyond the legal limit of twenty-five miles per hour. "Very worried about you, but fine."

"I suppose Mom's been pretending to be worried about me, too." Edie sounded bitter and I didn't blame her. Her arms were crossed tightly. If you believed in body language, I guess it would be easy to figure out that the mere mention of Mom upset her.

I tried to be noncommittal. "Your mom has some problems and can't see that she's hurt you." I made a left, tires squealing.

"Yeah, all she wanted to do was hurt my dad."

I had to question Edie sooner or later about the killer. This was good a starting place as any. "When did you realize she'd lied to you about your dad?"

Edie looked over at me, her long, unkempt blond hair half-covering her face. "That first week. When we were in Kentucky, I overheard her telling my grandma and aunts about what she did." She ran a hand through her hair, pushing it back.

"Edie, if you knew, why didn't you contact your dad before now?" We were heading toward the highway now, the one that ran down the coast.

She looked straight ahead and started blinking rapidly. "At first I figured Mom needed me and that's why she took me away. Later, when I wanted to contact Daddy, there was never any place I could do it. I tried to call him when I stayed over at Rachel's, but he was never home and he doesn't have an answering machine. He has a beeper, but I lost the number."

I took a deep breath. "Edie, I know this isn't the

place to ask, but I need to know some unpleasant things. Can you talk about it?''

"Sure, I have to sometime." When I glanced over at her, she looked about ready to cry. "Rachel's dead, isn't she?''

There wasn't any other way to tell her except straight. "Yeah, she is.''

"I wasn't sure when I saw her there, and I ran away. I was afraid to go home. Mom wouldn't have been able to protect me, and I was afraid to go to the police. I'd heard Herb and Bobbie talking about his condo in Nahant, and he showed her the key. He was working at his shop on Saturday and I snuck in and lifted the key when he wasn't looking.''

"Why were you afraid to go to the police?''

"I was afraid they'd take me back to Mom." She looked at her hands, tears streaming silently down her face. "I felt so selfish about leaving Rachel there, but I was scared.''

I tried to imagine how I'd feel, helpless, afraid that the police would send me back to my mother, wondering if anyone would believe me.

"Tell me about Rachel and you. What happened?''

"We were coming home from school. Rachel's debate club had been canceled because the teacher was sick." She started to chew on a hangnail. "I was already planning to run away that night, and Rachel was going to help me get back to Daddy.''

"Yes, I know. I'm sorry, but I had to read your diary.''

Edie shrugged. "I wrote that, maybe hoping that Mom would see what was happening to her. I was tired of taking care of her." She stopped talking suddenly, and when I looked over, she was looking out the passenger-side mirror.

"What's wrong, Edie?"

"The car behind you is coming up on us awful fast."

Headlights exploded into my rearview mirror, and I barely had time to swerve to the right. Big mistake. The vehicle came shoulder to shoulder with my Corsica and started nudging me toward the edge of the road. I noticed it was a pickup. Big help in who the killer was—both Blount and Cooper owned pickups, and it was too dark to distinguish between black and dark blue.

"I hope your seat belt's fastened, kid," I said. "It could be a bumpy ride."

Then I felt the truck hit against my door, and my stomach lurched. I swerved again and the pickup swerved right with me, as if it was stuck to us like Krazy Glue. Then came the crunch of metal against metal as our attacker pushed us off the road. I tried to put on the brakes, but my foot slipped. I tried again and succeeded. The Corsica's tires squealed as the antilock brakes took hold, and when I looked over at Edie, she had braced her feet against the dashboard.

I just closed my eyes. There wasn't much else you can do when you're being forced off the road. I just hoped the Corsica wouldn't plow into something hard.

It seemed to take a long time to stop, but when we finally did, the car was sitting at an angle. The driver's-side airbag had inflated, and I was having trouble seeing over it. I pushed at it until I could see that Edie was all right.

I heard a car door open and knew it was the killer. Looking around, I noticed that we were still ten miles away from Lynn.

"Edie," I whispered, "are you all right?"

"Yes, but I'm scared. We're going to die, aren't we?"

"Look, I can't get out of here without going through your side." I told her what to do while I tried to extricate myself from the airbag.

A few moments later, I heard the crunch of shoes on gravel. "Edie," a familiar voice called out, "I know you're in there! Come on out."

I undid my seat belt and worked on pushing the airbag aside. Then I slid through the open space between the bucket seats so I could get out the back passenger-side door. Meanwhile, Edie had scrunched down in her seat with her feet resting on the partly open door. I watched the man approach from my place in the backseat. The door suddenly swung open with the force of Edie's legs and caught the man in the chest and midsection, knocking him backward.

"Oof!"

"Go on, now," I urged quietly. "Get out of the car and find a hiding place somewhere out there. I'll call for you when it's safe." Like I was going to get out of this alive.

I heard Edie get out and run, then watched as the killer struggled to get up. I looked around for a weapon and found nothing handy. Taking a deep breath, I got out of the car. I'd lost the flashlight somewhere back near the condo.

In the glare of the Corsica's headlights, Joe Blount stood up, his face a mask of rage. In his hand, he had a bottle of J&B. Most of it was gone.

He shouted into the darkness. "Edie!"

"It's over, Joe," I said quietly. I could hear a roaring in my ears and tried to focus on the danger in front of me.

He turned around to look at me. "Whaddya mean, it's over? I got you an' Edie here. I can take care of both of you."

I had to keep him talking, keep him from going after Edie. "It was an accident, wasn't it, Joe?"

He blinked. "I don't know. I don't remember." Blount scrunched up his large features with the effort.

Since Edie hadn't been able to tell me what happened, I took a wild stab at the events. "You met the girls as you were coming out of Bobbie's place, right?"

"Yeah," he said, his expression vague. "They were running away and wanted a ride to Route One. We were in the car when I suggested they stay at my place just for the night to think it over." He stopped and stared at the empty road. I was hoping a car would drive by, but it was as desolate as the Great Salt Flats.

It was time to prompt him. "When you woke up, Rachel was dead." He nodded, his eyes still searching for something. "And Edie came in, saw you, saw Rachel, and ran away."

"I knew I must have done something bad the night before," Blount said, "but I couldn't remember how it happened. Then Edie came in, and ran away. I had to go after her, stop her.''

That was why he had passed the lie detector test. He'd had so much to drink that he'd blacked out and couldn't remember the night before. When he was asked if he'd killed Rachel, his vital signs didn't jump when he said no. But Blount realized that he couldn't count on passing the test without some help. And David's comment about using a tack to make answers consistent on the test reminded me that I'd seen Blount remove a tack from his shoe. This was how Blount passed the test.

"Sh-she didn't let me explain," Blount said. He took another swig from his bottle.

"What's to explain?" I said. "You buried the body in your yard then went looking for Edie. But she'd already gone into hiding. She knew you'd come after her. Why did you dig up Rachel?"

"If Edie went to the police, they would have found the body. Better to dump it somewhere away from my home."

Swaying slightly, he shook his head. "And now I have to take care of both of you." He finished the bottle and pushed against Edie's door, which closed with a final *thunk*. Then he whacked the bottom of his bourbon bottle against my car. I winced and had to bite my tongue to keep from saying, "Watch the Corsica, pal"—reminding myself that the driver's side was totaled now, anyway.

I moved away from the car into the ditch, muddling on in the dark, away from the road and into soft, pliable ground. *Great. I take self-defense lessons to be able to handle myself in any situation, and when I face this guy, I'll barely be able to stand.* My shoes sank into the sand as I drew him farther away from our cars. I was hoping Edie would find her way back to the cars and flag down someone—if anyone ever used this road.

Then it came to me: We weren't far from the ocean. That was the roaring I'd heard before. Sure enough, as I crested a small sand dune, I could see the ocean. Blount was practically breathing down my back and I sprinted on, looking for something, a piece of driftwood, a bottle, anything.

I got a pins-and-needles feeling on the back of my neck and turned around in time to see Blount swing his broken bottle at me. I automatically stepped away and tried to grab on to his wrist, but he pulled away from me, leaving a wicked bloody wound on my forearm that stung like hell. I yelped and jumped back, toppling over onto the sand.

He came at me again, that drunken gleam in his eye, the bottle held aloft as he swung it down with full force. I rolled away, getting sand in the cut. It was like applying sandpaper to an open wound. I tried to stand up, but he came at me again. I went into a crouch, and Blount tripped over me and went sailing into a sand dune. I got up and he was still laying there.

I waited for a few minutes to make sure he wasn't going to get up again, then cautiously approached him and used one foot to turn him over. He'd fallen on his own jagged bottle. He was still alive, but there was a lot of blood.

I felt Edie come up next to me. "Is he—?"

I stepped between Edie and Blount's body. "Don't look. Let's go." We headed for the vehicles, hoping one of them would get us into Lynn or Swampscott.

TWENTY-TWO

EDIE DUG OUT a grubby bandanna from her pocket and we wrapped the gash in my arm.

"You okay?" she asked. I glanced in the Corsica's side-view mirror and noted that I looked like shit. Nausea crept up in my throat and I took a deep breath to push it back down.

I managed a smile. "Yeah, I'm fine. Let's get out of here."

My car wouldn't start, but Blount's pickup did, and we peeled out of there, heading for Lynn. When we got there, the desk sergeant listened to my story and was kind enough to contact Holmes and Mac-Millan without any further questions. MacMillan, in turn, contacted Ev and Earlene.

The desk sergeant also dispatched a unit and an ambulance to pick up Blount, and a tow truck was sent out for the remains of my car. A police unit drove me to the hospital and had my wound attended to—disinfected, five stitches, and wrapped in clean gauze—then I was brought back to the station. It was the fastest emergency room service I'd ever gotten. I made a mental note to have a police unit drive me to the ER every time I was sick or wounded, which I hoped wouldn't happen often.

When I got back to the station, Ev was already there with Mac and Holmes. I figured they must have had the sirens going and the dome lights on the entire way. While I talked to the police, Ev and Edie were shown into a private room to have some time alone.

I was slumped in a chair, weary to the bone, when the news came in that Joe Blount was in critical condition at the hospital.

"Wow, I didn't think I did that much damage," I said.

"It was a gut wound, but the doctors say he'll make it," Holmes said.

"That's good," I replied. "I haven't killed anyone this week, and I want to keep my record clean."

"This isn't funny, Angela," Holmes said.

I rubbed my face and blinked my bloodshot eyes a few times. "I know it isn't. That was called dry humor, Rob. I get that way when it's past my bedtime."

"What the hell did you think you were doing?" MacMillan asked, as he invaded my personal space. I tried not to take it personally. "You went out to an empty condo unit in the middle of nowhere without contacting us."

"Look, I know you guys have to do this, but can I just take my toys after this interview and go home?"

Holmes gave me an ambiguous look. "Answer the question."

I waved him away. "I know, I know. We'll be here all night if I don't get serious. I didn't know it was an empty condo unit, and I didn't know Blount was following me. All I was thinking about was finding Edie for my client. Look, guys, I was almost killed, and so was Edie."

Ev came into the office. His arm was around Edie

in a protective manner. I couldn't keep from smiling as I watched father and daughter together. I wondered if Ev knew how strong Edie was, and I wondered if I would ever have a daughter of my own. What would she be like at fourteen? I hoped she'd be a lot like Edie.

"We'd like to go now; Edie can give you her statement in the morning."

Mac looked sharply at Ev. Then his eyes met Holmes's, and I detected an imperceptible nod between them. "Yeah. We'll talk to her in the morning."

They were turning back to me to ask more questions when Ev said, "That includes Angie."

MacMillan stepped back and Holmes stood up. They looked at each other for a fraction of a second before MacMillan replied, "Come to the station in Revere tomorrow, Angela, and we'll continue where we left off."

We had just passed through the Lynn police station doors when we met Earlene coming up the steps. She wore a pair of faded jeans and a dirty white blouse. Her hair wasn't combed but had just been pushed out of her eyes.

"Edie!" Her red eyes were from drinking, not from crying.

"Mom," Edie said softly. Ev tried to keep hold of her, but Edie gently detached herself and hugged her mother.

Over Edie's shoulder Earlene gave Ev a defiant look.

I noticed Ev's hands had become fists, and he took a step toward them. "Edie," he said in a rough voice.

I moved over to Ev and put my hand on his arm. He tore his gaze away from mother and daughter and looked down at me. I shook my head silently. He seemed to deflate.

Edie backed away from her mother and returned to her father's side.

"You look fine, baby," Earlene said, holding out a hand and pointedly ignoring Ev's presence. "Come on home, baby."

A tear slipped down Edie's cheek. "I can't take care of you anymore, Mom. I'm going home with Daddy."

"But, Edie, I promise—"

I turned to Earlene. "I think you'd better go now."

She hit out at my arm, but I easily evaded her. Her face twisted in anger, and her eyes burned with a feverish light. "She's my daughter, too, you stinking whore! What d'you know about it?"

I took a deep breath. She stood there, swaying. Ev and Edie had stepped around me and were headed to the car.

"We'll wait for you," Ev muttered to me. "Thanks."

I turned back to Earlene. "I don't know what to say to you, Earlene. You've got no rights left to that child. She's been through enough this past week, don't you think?"

Tears were streaming down her face. Her voice was rough with emotion. "She's my daughter, too," she repeated.

The problem was, I couldn't tell if her feelings were about losing Edie because she loved her or because Ev had won some twisted contest between the two of them. I was too tired to stand there and argue with this whiny, self-absorbed woman. I turned around and left her standing on the precinct steps.

As Ev pulled the car away, I caught a glimpse of a forlorn Earlene sinking onto the steps, openly howling in hurt and anger.

Edie fell asleep in the backseat. On the way to my apartment, I turned to Ev and told him what I'd told Earlene. "I don't want that woman to ever come near my child again," he said in a harsh tone that left no room for speculation. I fell silent until we got back to my place.

I convinced Ev that it would be best for Edie if they stayed over at my place. I let them use my apartment and I went a flight down to sleep in Rosa's guest bedroom.

IT WAS ABOUT nine when I woke up, later than I usually sleep, but it had been something like 3:00 a.m. when we crawled into my apartment building. I thought about going upstairs to see if they were up, but I looked out the window and saw Ev's car still out front. I decided to give them another hour.

I briefly wondered where he'd gotten the car on such short notice. As far as I knew, he'd been cabbing it and using the subway to get around. I figured it was probably borrowed from the marine corps recruiting office.

Rosa was up, and as I staggered out of the bedroom, the smell of coffee brewing led me to the kitchen. I was wearing the boxers and a sleeveless T-shirt that I'd brought downstairs last night, but I'd forgotten a robe. Rosa was sitting at the kitchen table, reading the *Globe*. She looked up, her eyes widening at the sight of my bandaged arm.

"Morning, Sarge. Rough night last night?"

I gave her a brief account of what happened while I poured myself a cup of thick, black coffee.

"Cream?" She indicated the half-pint carton on the table.

I waved it away. "Give me a break. I've been drinking it black since I was fifteen."

"Sarge, I've—" She stopped, seeming to search for whatever it was she wanted to say. She looked up. "I've decided to go back to school."

"Great!"

Rosa blinked. "You're not mad?"

"Why would I be?" I asked. A hurt look came over her face. I remedied my quick response. "I mean, you can still work part-time, can't you? I get a lot of repo and insurance work."

Her face cleared. "I don't think I can do it."

I frowned. "You've done fine these last few days, Rosa." I suddenly realized I'd miss her if she decided not to work with me.

She lowered her eyes. "I didn't mind the insurance work, but I repossessed a few cars, too. I'm not sure I'm cut out for that type of work."

"Come on, Rosa, you know the type of people who get their cars repo'ed."

She looked puzzled. "What do you mean?"

"Deadbeats."

"These people aren't deadbeats. One of them was a friend of mine from the university. He missed a couple of payments because he lost his job and had to choose between paying his rent or his car." She stood up to get more coffee, and gave me a reproachful look. "I'm surprised at your intolerance, Sarge."

I waved her away. "You don't know what you're talking about."

She turned around and gave me a hard stare. "No, you don't know what *you're* talking about. Maybe there are people like what you've described. But my friends are hard-working people who want to better themselves, and I won't be able to do a repo without thinking of my friend, who now doesn't have a car to visit his aging mother in New Hampshire." She put her coffee cup down with enough force to make me jump. Coffee sloshed over the sides onto the bright yellow tabletop. Then Rosa leaned over me. "So if you want me to continue working for you on a part-time basis, you'll have to take me on those terms."

My little sister, the mild one, on a rampage. Wow! I decided not to tell her that all the deadbeats whose cars were repo'ed always had a poor aging mother somewhere.

She narrowed her eyes. "What are you grinning about?"

I shrugged. "It's just refreshing to see you stand up for yourself. And, yes, I can be an intolerant bitch sometimes. I'll take you on your terms."

"Good." She sat down, a look of satisfaction on her face, and sipped her coffee. "I start back to school in January."

"What's your major this time?"

"Art history."

A few minutes later, I heard Ev coming softly down the stairs. Edie was talking and Ev was trying to shush her. I opened Rosa's door. Ev stopped in midstep.

"Leaving so soon?" I leaned on the doorframe and crossed my arms.

There was a sheepish look on Ev's handsome face, but he covered it up quite well by running his eyes over my body. "So, that's what you sleep in?"

Rosa came to the door. "Coffee, anyone?" Edie walked in. She didn't look happy. Ev's face reddened and he came in reluctantly.

"We can only stay a minute," he said. "We have to get to the hotel and pack up. Washington needs me back in California."

I stared at him, but he avoided my eyes. Edie looked ready to cry. She excused herself and went into the living room to watch TV.

"What about visiting the police in Revere?" I asked.

"We can take care of it once we get back home."

"So you're going to leave me here to face the music alone."

He gave me a sharp look but said nothing. I had plenty to say, but I needed to take a break. I have a habit of shooting my mouth off around those who weren't brought up in an Italian family, and they always react badly. I excused myself and went into the other room where Edie was watching some talk show with a smiling gargoyle of a woman bantering with some idiotic-looking guy who had an annoying laugh.

Edie looked up at me. "How you doing?" I asked, touching her shoulder.

She shrugged. "Okay, I guess."

I sat down next to her. "Can you tell me what happened, what made you run?"

"I saw Rachel and Joe together, only Rachel was—" She broke off and swallowed hard.

"Take your time," I said. "If it's too hard for you—"

She shook her head mutely and started playing with her hair. "I've got to talk about it. Dad doesn't think so, but I know I have to. I'm gonna miss Rachel. It's all my fault. If I hadn't missed Daddy so much—"

I took her chin and turned her face toward me until our eyes met. "It's not your fault. You wanted to go home and Rachel was your best friend. It sounds as if Joe Blount doesn't remember what happened."

Edie squeezed her eyes shut for a moment, swallowed hard, then took a deep breath. "We met Joe outside my house. He looked real upset. And I could tell he'd been drinking."

"Rachel's parents said that she had a debate meeting on Fridays, but you told me yesterday that the meeting was canceled," I said.

Edie nodded. "Like I said before, Rachel knew her parents didn't like my mom, so we decided to pretend the meeting had happened. That way, she could come over to my house for the afternoon."

"What happened next?"

"We talked to Joe, and he said I could stay at his place for the night. Rachel didn't want me to go to Joe's alone. So Joe agreed to drive Rachel home and take me to Route One in the morning. He seemed okay, even though he'd been drinking." Tears trav-

eled down her face and she sniffed. I went in the
bathroom and got a box of tissues.

Edie took one and blew her nose. "Rachel and I
went to bed early. We didn't like it there, but I finally
fell asleep. When I woke up in the morning, Rachel
wasn't in the room. I figured she'd gone in the
kitchen or bathroom and I looked in both rooms. I
saw lots of beer cans in the living room, but Rachel
wasn't there, either."

"That leaves the bedroom," I prompted her.
"Joe's room."

Edie nodded. "She was there." She started sobbing. I gave her another tissue. "And she wasn't
moving. And he was bent over her. I must have made
a sound because he looked up at me, and I knew that
if I didn't get out of there then, I never would. So I
turned and ran."

I could hear the murmur of voices in the next
room. Ev's was raised slightly, Rosa's was soothing.

I put my arm around Edie and hugged her. "You
did a good thing, honey."

She shrugged. "Dad wants to go home. He doesn't
want me to have to go through any more. He says
we should just forget everything."

I was doing a slow burn, but I managed to push it
down. "What do you think?"

For a second, all the pain flashed across her face,
then she looked up at me with resolve. "I think Joe
needs to go away for a long time. And I'm the only
one who can do it."

I squeezed her shoulder. Ev came into the living
room. His voice was harsh. "Come on, Edie. We've
got to go."

I stood up and faced him. "So you're going to just run away."

His face was impassive as he studied me coldly. "What would you know about it? You don't have children."

I threw him a cool smile. "But I've known plenty of them. I was one once, you know."

Impatience flashed across his features. "Cut the crap, Matelli. I don't have time for this."

"Maybe you should ask Edie what she thinks is best for her."

"So now you're playing amateur psychologist?"

I crossed my arms. "It's better than playing Major Dickhead."

He opened his mouth to say something but shut it quickly.

"Daddy, you've always told me to do the right thing." Edie's face was still a little puffy from crying, but the tears had stopped. She was standing next to me now.

"What is this, a mutiny?" Ev frowned. "I know what's best for you."

Edie stuck her chin out. "And that includes never seeing Mom again?"

He looked at her thoughtfully and rubbed his forehead.

Edie spoke again. "Daddy, I know Mom didn't do the right thing. But I wasn't exactly helpless. I didn't call you at first because it was great not to have any rules to follow. And Mom needed me more than you did." She went over to him and gave him a hug. He stiffened for a moment, then relaxed and put an arm around her. "I love you, Daddy, but sometimes it's hard to be your daughter. Let me do the right thing. Stop protecting me.''

Ev blinked several times and held her at arm's length to look in her eyes. ''Don't you know yet, Edie? I need you, too.'' He bent down and kissed the top of his daughter's head. ''Okay, sweetheart. We'll go to the police station, and you can give your statement. And if you're needed, we'll get you back here for the trial.''

She pulled away from him. ''And I can see Mom every now and then?''

He hesitated and threw me a glance. I just raised my eyebrows. ''Don't look at me. Remember? I've never had children.''

''If and when your mom gets some help for her problems, but I won't let you stay with her.''

Edie looked over at me. ''Maybe I could stay with Angie when I come to visit Mom.''

I was reluctant to say yes, but Rosa apparently wasn't. ''Oh, that should be fine. I'm sure Angie would be happy to look after her.''

''Thanks, Rosa,'' I said through gritted teeth. She patted my shoulder and left the room.

Ev was looking amused. ''We'll see.''

I saw them to the front door downstairs and told Ev to relay the message to Holmes and MacMillan that I would be coming in a little later this afternoon. Edie gave me a hug and a thanks, then bounded down the front steps.

Ev paused at the top of the steps and walked back to me. ''By the way, did I say thanks, Angie?''

I shook my head mutely, a smile on my lips. He took me in his arms and we kissed—a long, heartfelt kiss that left me wanting more. He stepped back from it and looked into my eyes. "Then from the bottom of my heart, thank you, Angie."

I looked away from him, a grin threatening to crack the glower I had perfected. "Get outta here."

When he was out of earshot, I said under my breath, "About damn time he thanked me."

I was getting ready to go back up to my apartment when Rosa came out of her place and locked the door. I mimicked her voice. "Oh, yes, Ev, Angie would be happy to look after Edie."

Rosa grinned. "Ev sure is nice, isn't he?" There was a twinkle in her eye. I chose to ignore it, doing my best to glare at her. She didn't seem to notice as she bounced down the steps. "See you later, Sarge. I gotta register for the next term."

TWENTY-THREE

I SPENT the rest of the morning in the Revere police station with MacMillan and Holmes. They were a little more civil to me this morning. In fact, they were downright friendly. They only had me go over my story half a dozen times before they were satisfied that I was telling the truth.

"So what's going to happen to Blount?" I asked.

Holmes was doodling on a pad. "He's in intensive care right now, but the doctors say he'll make it through. And then he goes to trial."

"What about Herb Cooper?"

MacMillan shrugged. "The girl insists that she crept into his shop and lifted his key while he was in the back."

I gave him my best you-don't-really-buy-that look. "What?" he asked. "What am I supposed to do? You don't believe her?"

"No more than you," I replied. "No one can creep into that shop. When you open the door, there's a bell that rings loud and clear."

Holmes and MacMillan looked at each other. "Why would she protect him?" Mac asked.

"Look, Angela, maybe he knew she was there," Holmes said. "But Edie insists that he didn't. Maybe he was planning something with her, or maybe he was just being a good friend. He saw how she lived, he knew her mother. Maybe he thought he was doing her a favor."

"Either way," MacMillan added, "it's not our department. They're sticking to their stories."

So I shrugged it off. There wasn't anything I could do, either. I ran into the McCarthys as I was leaving. They were just coming in. Diane had puffy, bloodshot eyes, and the tip of her nose was red. Larry had his arm around her, supporting her. It was as if they had reversed roles. At their house on Sunday night, it had been Diane who seemed to be the strong one and Larry who seemed to feel all the pain.

"We're very grateful to you, Miss Matelli," Larry said as he shook my hand.

"Yes, thank you for finding our daughter's killer," Diane said. I must have looked as blank as I felt because she added, "That nice Detective MacMillan told us you were instrumental in finding him."

"If we owe you anything extra…" Larry said.

I waved my hand, feeling a little guilty about taking their money. After all, I hadn't found Blount, he'd found me. "No, you don't owe me anything. In fact, I owe you a balance." I did some quick mental arithmetic to figure out what to give them back.

"No, we insist you keep the remainder as a bonus," Diane said as she shook my hand.

After they left, I didn't feel any better. Sure, I'd found Rachel's killer, but she was still dead. I was providing a service and they seemed happy enough to receive it, but it wouldn't bring Rachel back to life. I thought about it all the way over to Earlene's house, and by the time I was knocking at her door, I'd decided that it wasn't my fault Rachel was dead.

Callous, but true. I was sorry she was gone; I hadn't known her while she was alive, but I had a feeling I would have liked her. I thought back to Edie suggesting that she come stay with me until her mother had proven herself, and I started to look forward to her visit.

Earlene answered the door. She was wearing a grubby, pale-yellow bathrobe and looked like she'd been crying. When she saw it was me, she left the door open and turned back toward the living room without a word.

"I suppose you've come to tell me that Ev and Edie have left for California," she said dully.

"They have. And Edie said she wanted to come out and visit you for the next holiday."

Earlene perked up. "Sh-she does?"

I gave her a severe look. "Under certain circumstances."

She had taken out a used tissue from the pocket of her bathrobe and was dabbing at her tears ineffectually. "What do you mean?"

I outlined what Edie, Ev, and I had agreed upon. "You have to enter AA or some other group. You have to show improvement. You must be willing to see Edie on her terms. Right now, that means that when she comes here, she'll stay with me, and your visits will be supervised."

Earlene's face had grown harder with each passing moment. She folded her arms. "This is all Ev's doing, isn't it? He just wants to control her and me."

I stood up. I was tired of tears and recriminations. "No, dammit. Those are Edie's rules. I heard her say it. Ev didn't want you to ever see her again. She

convinced him that you need her. She loves you, but
Ev is a better parent. You know you have a problem;
you just won't admit it. Is it more important to be
right than to have a relationship with your daughter?" I dug around in my purse and handed her one
of my cards. "Call me when you've made a decision,
and I'll put you in touch with Ev."

There was a moment when her chin trembled, and
I thought her stubbornness would get the better of
her. But she finally reached out and took the card.

I WENT TO THE OFFICE to catch up on some paperwork until five, then headed home. When I stepped
in the front door, I noticed that Sophia's door was
open. I knocked and walked in. Some wonderful
smell emanated from the kitchen, and I wondered
what she was cooking. Sophia popped her head out
the kitchen door. "Angie! Come on in."

"What are you cooking?" My stomach rumbled,
anticipating food. I realized I'd only had coffee in
the morning and a small chicken parmesan sub this
afternoon.

She blushed. "It's a new recipe—chicken curry
with sour cream. Dave bugged me to try it." My
sister, the modern version of Donna Reed.

From the living room, I could hear squeals of plea-
sure from the kids, then a male adult voice. I walked
in and Dave, who had sprawled his lanky frame all
over the floor, was concentrating on a game of Triv-
ial Pursuit for kids that was spread out on the cheap
coffee table. Michael and Stephanie noticed me first.

"Aunt Angie, we're beating the pants off him,"
said Michael.

"Hey, Ange," Dave called out. "Want to join me against these two midget intellectuals here?"

I held up my hands. "Oh, I don't know...."

Sophia was wiping her hands with a dishtowel. "We have plenty of food. Why don't you stay, Angie?" This from Sophia, the sister from hell?

I made my decision. I didn't know what tomorrow would bring—a marriage between these two completely different people or a painful breakup. But I couldn't run their lives for them. And that curry sure smelled good. I had a bottle of wine upstairs in my refrigerator that would go nicely.

"Yeah, why don't I?"

From the bestselling author of
Shocking Pink and *Fortune*

ERICA SPINDLER

THEY OPENED THEIR DOOR TO A STRANGER...AND THEIR DREAM BECAME A NIGHTMARE

Julianna Starr has chosen Kate and Richard Ryan to be *more* than the parents of her child. Obsessed with Richard, Julianna molds herself in Kate's image and insinuates herself into the couple's life, determined to tear their perfect marriage apart. But the nightmare has only begun. Because Julianna is not alone. From her dark past comes a man of unspeakable evil.... Now no one is safe—not even the innocent child Kate and Richard call their own.

CAUSE FOR ALARM

SPINDLER DELIVERS "A HIGH ADVENTURE OF LOVE'S TRIUMPH OVER TWISTED OBSESSION." —*Publishers Weekly*

On sale mid-February 1999 wherever paperbacks are sold!

MIRA

Look us up on-line at: http://www.mirabooks.com   MES497

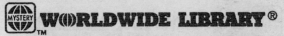
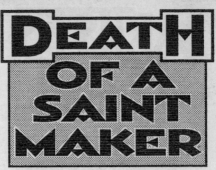

WORLDWIDE LIBRARY®

ARTIST'S PROOF

GORDON COTLER

A SID SHALE MYSTERY

STILL LIFE

Nothing could have persuaded ex-NYPD cop turned artist Sid Shale to get back into the investigative groove. Until Cassie Brennan's murder.

The victim had posed several times for Sid...in the nude. To save his own neck, Sid starts sifting through the sands of Cassie's last days—from the distraught boyfriend to the shady restaurateur who hired her as a cleaning lady—uncovering a motive for murder as primal as it is tragic.

Available January 1999 at your favorite retail outlet.

W☉RLDWIDE LIBRARY®

Award-winning author of *The Harry Chronicles*

ALLAN PEDRAZAS
ANGEL'S COVE

A HARRY RICE MYSTERY

Following a frantic call from his bartender, Carla, private investigator and beachside pub owner Harry Rice makes an all-night drive to the small coastal town of Angel's Cove.

The victim is Carla's dad. Harry's probe and his presence put him on unfriendly terms with the local police, the medical examiner and the fish militia. But that doesn't stop him from exposing a billion-dollar deal where murder is just another way of doing business.

Available February 1999 at your favorite retail outlet.

Look us up on-line at: http://www.worldwidemystery.com   WAP302